*Marion Manville Pope*

# Up the Matterhorn in a Boat

Marion Manville Pope

## Up the Matterhorn in a Boat

ISBN/EAN: 9783954272365
Erscheinungsjahr: 2012
Erscheinungsort: Bremen, Deutschland

© maritimepress in Europäischer Hochschulverlag GmbH & Co. KG, Fahrenheitstr. 1, 28359 Bremen. Alle Rechte beim Verlag und bei den jeweiligen Lizenzgebern.

www.maritimepress.de | office@maritimepress.de

Bei diesem Titel handelt es sich um den Nachdruck eines historischen, lange vergriffenen Buches. Da elektronische Druckvorlagen für diese Titel nicht existieren, musste auf alte Vorlagen zurückgegriffen werden. Hieraus zwangsläufig resultierende Qualitätsverluste bitten wir zu entschuldigen.

"'THE MATTERHORN!' CRIED I."
(See page 101.)

# Up
# The  Matterhorn
# In  a  Boat

by

## Marion Manville Pope

New York
The Century Co.
1897

TO
AUNT LOUISA
BEST AND TRUEST OF FRIENDS
KINDEST AND MOST GENEROUS
OF SOULS

# ILLUSTRATIONS

# UP THE MATTERHORN
# IN A BOAT

# UP THE MATTERHORN IN A BOAT

## I

"I AM going up there, but not à la the present mode — strung on a rope with guides and porters like beads on a string. I shall go in a balloon."

" Any time scheduled for starting ? "

" No," said Hill, reflectively ; " I 've got to go back to Paris first.   Would you like to join me ? "

" Where for — Paris or Mont Blanc ? "

" Mont Blanc."

" In a balloon ? "

" Yes, or a sky-boat."

" Safe ? "

" As climbing."

" All right ; let me know in time, and I 'll go."

There the matter ended—at least I supposed it did, for I had not taken it seriously at all.   We had been sitting on the hotel veranda, smoking, and looking at the

"THE PRESENT MODE."

mountains.   I expected to visit Mont Blanc in a sky-boat about as much as I did Mars in a similar craft; but I was astonished to hear from my chance friend Hill a few weeks afterward, and to be reminded of the above conversation.   There were some newspaper clippings in his letter, and from them I gleaned that Hill was an aëronaut and experimenter generally. This he had never even hinted to me, and I liked him all the better now for his reticence. He said little, but what he did say was generally worth hearing; and the ninth letter of our alphabet would never have been worn flat and smooth in a few hours by him, providing it was in type. I accepted the clippings as a sort of introduction to the skill of the man, and I felt that they were not offered in a spirit of vainglorious pride, much as it might have been justified by the flattering tone of the paragraphs. He knew, naturally, that I would hardly want to go sky-boating without knowing something about the qualifications of the pilot, who would probably be captain and crew, too, like the survivor of the "good ship *Nancy Bell.*" Looked at in this way, the clippings were eminently satisfactory as references; so I accepted the invitation, and started back for Chamonix.

I arrived there two days before the time specified by Hill, and on the evening of the second I was again sitting on the veranda where we had held our previous conversation. It was summer, and according to the papers it was pretty warm in Europe. There was a full moon, and as I looked at its round face peering over the ghostly summits of the eternal snows, I wondered how nature contrived to get up any heat to speak of in the same house with what might be called that tremendous cold-storage system. And as I sat there smoking, and meditating on Hill and mountain, there came a great creaking and hallooing up the street; and presently two carts appeared, attended by a fair following of youth and age, and a good exhibit of French vocabulary. The whole outfit stopped before the hotel, and a dozen men at once began to drag from the first vehicle a limp and shapeless wad of something that bulged in places, and caved in in others, and sagged everywhere like a big net full of the season's best catch. This extraordinary spectacle was what had evidently drawn the multitude, and its significance at once dawned upon me. Here was the sky-boat! I

"TWO CARTS APPEARED."

got down to the street just as Hill came hurrying up.

"Hallo!" said he; "on time, eh? Here, you; no fooling with that boat until I show you how." He had started to shake hands with me, but broke the action off as abruptly as he did the verbal salutation. The next minute he was around the other side of the second vehicle, repeating his instructions in French.

I examined the craft before me as well as I could in the moonlight, and discovered that it was made of metal, — aluminium, I afterward learned, — pointed at both ends like a racing-shell, but very much broader and deeper. It was as deep in proportion as a life-boat, and, used as a water-craft, would have seated six or eight people comfortably without any crowding, although there was a floor, or a sort of lower deck, built midway across it, forming a tiny hold below. Chains were attached where the oar-locks should have been, and also at prow and stern, while directly beneath each of these, lying flat along the sides and at both ends, — those at the ends somewhat resembling rudders, only they also lay as flat and as close to the boat as possible, — were six curious contrivances, looking precisely like folding fans, riveted on at the handles. These I rightly concluded to be connected with the steering-gear. But what chiefly aroused my wonderment was a small, fat cannon, or mortar, lying on the bottom of the boat, like the stump of a big cigar. This appeared to be of the same material as the boat itself, and putting my hand down on the rim in order to turn it over, I was surprised to find it fitted with a glass cover. On further inspection I discovered that this glass was a lens, and that back of it were other lenses, or else some brilliant, sparkling stuff, half filling the body of the cone.

"What is this machine?" I asked. "It looks like a mortar for throwing shell, barring the glass lid; but I suppose it is n't a gun."

"Yes, it is," replied Hill, coming around to my side for a minute, and taking it out of my hands. "This is a light-gun. We attach a fuse to it, as it were; we put the finger of electricity on the trigger,—although we can use a tallow dip in case of necessity,—and then we aim it at whatever we can't see.   Usually, you know, you aim a gun at something you can see; but this is a combination of camera, telescope, cannon, and magic-lantern.   You just train this chap on nothing in the dark, and watch him fire big shells of light at it.   I tell you, it 's great!"

"I should think it might be," said I; "but what are these?" and I laid my hand on one of the big fans folded along the rail.

"Oh, those are our fins.  We simply spread them in order to tack.  They run by electricity, and help us to swim—in the air."

Before I could make any comment he dropped the light-gun back into the boat, and hurriedly detached himself from the conversation.  It was useless to ask him any more questions then, but I had my doubts about the feasibility of using gas in those high altitudes; and after the boat and the balloon were stowed away for the night, and Hill had his mind back to earth again temporarily, I asked:

"What is the temperature up around Mont Blanc?"

"Well," said he, slowly, "it's pretty cold. I expect it needs a spirit-thermometer to register up there at some seasons."

"That's what I thought," said I. "It seems reasonable to suppose that those old noses of the Alps are about the coldest spots we have on this mundane sphere. What's to hinder the gas in the balloon from congealing when you get up several thousand feet?"

"Electricity."

"Oh?"

"Yes. But if it should freeze, you just figure out how much more congealed gas weighs than the uncongealed variety. Is a pound of ice heavier than a pound of water?" There was a regular Yankee twinkle in his eyes for a minute, but presently he continued seriously: "As to the gas congealing, I suppose it might run the risk of that were it not for the fact that we shall counteract the influence of the cold by motion.   Do you know anything about the dynamical theory of heat?"

"Not much," said I, modestly.

"Well, you don't have to know 'much' to comprehend that when you leave the water running in the faucet on a cold night you prevent its freezing because you set it in motion.   It 's the vibration of particles of matter that keeps them from solidifying, because motion is the first principle of heat, or heat is motion, as you please.   Is that clear?"

"Perfectly."

"Very well; that is the dynamical theory of heat.   Don't you see that all we 've got to do is to keep the gas in that balloon churned up?   We are going to accomplish that with the aid of a little wheel, like a paddle-wheel, inside the balloon.   I attach it to the current from the storage-battery directly we get high enough to need it; and, you may depend upon it, the gas is not sitting down and congealing, or frosting its airy toes, so long as it 's kept on the move by the paddle."

"That sounds all right," said I; "but

where does the dynamical theory of heat come in with an ice-cream freezer?  You keep that churned up, and it freezes right along just the same."

"That 's a different application of energy," said he.  "According to my theory, we run no risk so long as we keep paddling."  I could say no more, but inwardly I hoped he had tested his theory before starting, for I felt that the atmosphere would be a pretty thin element to stand on with any exploded notions.  "You see," he went on, changing his subject, "while our quarters are rather small, — big as an English railway-compartment, though, and better facilities for heating, — we are going to be pretty comfortable.  In fact, the American does n't travel unless he is.  But, to begin with, as I said, we have electricity. We have the light-gun to fire ahead and see if the air is clear of rocks, and we shall cook by electricity.  If you can catch any fish as we sail, I 'll drop them right into the skillet; or if we run down any game, we can keep it frozen by hanging it over our stern, where it 's handy to cut off a slice now and then as we need it. It will be an economical way of housekeeping — no ice-bills, no trouble with refrigerators and plumbers, no water-bugs, no cock-roaches." He smiled as he spoke. "I have laid in a supply of canned goods, enough to last us six days, good liberal rations for appetites with an edge on them ; and all I ask of you is to bring yourself and flannels, instead of yourself and friends — although if anything should go wrong with our machinery, your flannels might be your best friends, after all."

"When do you expect to get off ?"

"Oh, about Thursday morning." It was then Tuesday night. "I 've nothing to do now but make the gas. We ought to get the *Cloud Queen* inflated in twenty-four hours, and then, hail to the unknown — to the unfound, but findable, realms of space! For those are the ports we sail for."

BEING in a community where they make avalanches a specialty is a great deal like being in a cyclone district or an earth-

quake country.  So far as my personal
experience goes, — it is all one whether I
am asleep or awake in the Alps neighbor-
hood or Japan, — the sound of a roar and a

"SAT UP WITH A JUMP."

rumble always has the same effect upon
me : it produces an earnest desire to stand
from under.   For this reason I awoke suddenly the next morning, and sat up in
bed with a jump.   Then I made ocean-

greyhound time over to the window, expecting to see the nearest mountain sliding sociably Chamonixward; but everything in nature was calm and serene. Art was at work under my window, though, with a whizz and a whir-r-r, and a sort of crescendo zee-e-e-e — the most diabolical row that human ears ever listened to. There was Hill standing over some sort of machine that was making the same noise in proportion to its size that a bluebottle fly does in proportion to his; and about him variously were jars and bottles and the balloon, the latter looking in the dim light not unlike a collapsed circus-tent at the end of the season. The machine was attached to the balloon, and was evidently generating gas after some novel method of Hill's own invention; for the old rag of a bag bulged and bubbled in a splotchy sort of dry-boiling. Heads were popping out of every window in sight by this time, two or three in some, — heads in nightcaps, and heads without, but every one with a facial frontage of astonishment, and every one talking, by the look of the mouths. They

"HEADS OUT OF WINDOWS."

might have been so many gnats in a saw-mill, though, for all the satisfaction they got out of that.

I dressed, and descended to the yard; but directly I met Hill, he seized me by the arm and drew me into the hotel.

"How did you sleep?" he inquired when the door was closed and he could be heard.

"First-class," said I, "until you started that row in the yard.  What, in the name of chaos, is *that* machine?"

I fancied there was rather a crafty gleam in his eyes, but he responded with seeming frankness:

"That?  Oh, that is the generator."

"What does it do for a living?  What is it — a motor?"

He looked at me for a minute after this compound question before he answered in a disgusted voice:

"A motor — that?  Did you ever hear a motor sing like that chap?"  He paused, and listened admiringly, as a fond father might to the lusty squalling of his first-born.  "Nothing the matter with those lungs, eh?"   I was forced to admit that they sounded healthy.  "The motor we are to take along is n't any bigger than your hat, and it might as well be asleep for all the noise it ever makes; but the generator — listen to it!"

I could n't help but listen, being in the vicinity.  "It seems to sing in several different keys at the same time," I ventured to say; but Hill ignored my remark. He tightened his grasp on my arm, and said confidentially:

"That is an atmospheric engine — that is to say, partly.  It 's a chemical engine, too.  Now I 've no doubt but you have heard people say all your life that atmospheric engines were the pet chimeras of cranks, have n't you? — cranks who were stalking perpetual motion?  It has always been contended by science that no practical application of ordinary atmospheric power could ever be made; that every scheme was bound to be a failure."  He dropped his voice to a solemn key.  "Does that sound like a failure?"

"If noise is any criterion to go by, it

sounds like a howling success," said I; "but what is it doing?"

"Why, it 's filling the balloon."

"With what — gas?"

"Yes; ammonia gas, largely; that and — something else — something that floats all right."

By this time we had reached the breakfast-room, where waiters were running distractedly around, trying to serve guests and keep track of the performance outside at the same time. As for the innkeeper himself, never had he been blessed with so precious a guest; never had his back rooms been so eagerly sought. The crowd in front drew visitors like a magnet, and the buzz and whir in the yard roared novelty to heaven. I heard him entreating Hill to make the show a permanent attraction, or at least to prolong the agony of inflating the *Cloud Queen* to a fortnight *à tout prix;* but Hill was obdurate, and the bag in the back yard passed slowly through the mud-geyser period of bubbling, and began to puff out symmetrically and show signs of floating on its own responsibility, like a scandal or a wildcat speculation scheme. As. the day advanced, and the wrinkles and crumples in the gown of the recumbent queen were smoothed out over the gas, it became apparent that what had appeared to be a badly mussed and dull-colored old fabric was in reality a changeable red-and-blue silk stuff of some tough weave. About noon I helped Hill carefully to unwrap a long roll containing a fine network of aluminium, a sort of chain-mail on a large scale, which we proceeded to draw over the top of the balloon as it lay billowing upon the ground in easy reach. The effect of these glittering chains over the softly luminous silk was wonderfully beautiful; and as the *Cloud Queen* began to take shape and substance, swaying gracefully from side to side as if to catch the sunbeams on her gorgeous robes, and ever rising gently heavenward, all the enthusiastic onlookers paid tribute to the royal lady by giving her a round of hearty applause. We all stood to admiring attention. Hill backed off, with his hands in his pockets and his hat on the back of his head.

"Looks just like a Yankee girl, eh?" he presently yelled at me. "Best of the kind made!"

I nodded. "I guess she's got a little drop of French blood in her."

"Not a bit! Her pa was yanked right out of Yankeedom; but, like all good American papas, he lets her buy her clothes in Paris."

He went over and touched a button or did something to the machine, and the noise suddenly ceased — so suddenly that it left everybody screaming something at everybody else in a pitch nicely adjusted to the previous uproar. Then he said to me:

"I 'll leave my man on duty, and we 'll go out and look at some of the places we are going to visit."

We found a young fellow comfortably seated at the hotel door, collecting a franc from each arrival, while the urbane inn-keeper washed his hands in the atmosphere before him, and enlarged upon the magnificence of the spectacle to be witnessed for the small price of admission. A man

"COLLECTING A FRANC."

whose house helped to make one side of the square, and whose rear windows looked into the yard, was letting his view at so much a head. This was canny enough to be Scotch. As we got well away, after elbowing a passage through the crowd, and looked back, we could see the top of the balloon swaying over the roofs of adjacent houses, like a great silver-veined poppy-bud rocking on its stem in the grass.

"It ought not to take over two hours more," said Hill, "to fill her, and then we are off. I should think we ought to get away by eight in the morning. We could have left all right to-night, but I like to have the inflation stand for a few hours before sailing. If there is any weakness in the fabric, it develops before we start, and can be attended to. Feel nervous?"

"No, not exactly; I have a sort of pioneering sensation, though."

"Well, that's appropriate. Now I am not going to talk shop to you, or try to explain the scientific whys and wherefores of things that a postgraduate course could not altogether elucidate; besides, I have n't the gift of expounding a twenty years' grind of study in fifteen minutes; but what I want to say is this: To all practical intents and purposes, we are going to be just as safe in my sky-ship as we would be on any seaworthy water-craft. I consider the *Cloud Queen* to be perfectly air-worthy. I 've got a lot of inventions that make her so, and we are not exposed to any more dangers afloat on the atmosphere than we are when afloat on the water. In fact, they are pretty much the same kind of dangers. For instance, if we spring a leak we sink. But we have life-preservers for the thin element as well as for the thicker. All you will have to do in such an event will be to keep your head and spread a parachute. Of course when you land you will have to take your chances — as you would at sea. I can't guarantee that you will descend on the roof of a first-class hotel with hot and cold water, gas, and all modern improvements at a reasonable rate —'no extra charge for candles.' If I could, I should be as infallible as the promise of dividends on a life-insurance. 'Now you 've got your pointer on springing a leak. The next danger we might be exposed to is another of the same sort you meet at sea, with modifications. We might run into something; but I calculate there is not more than one chance in ninety-nine million of our running into anything of our own size and kind, so there we have a decided advantage over steamers. Of course we may strike a snag or a crag, but there again we have a remedy. All we 've got to do in that event is to throw out a grappling-iron and catch on. There 's bound to be something to hold on to the moment we leave the air. You can't get a good hold on air, although it 's just as satisfying as trying to get a good firm grip on water, so there again you are just as well off as if you were at sea. And here is another advantage: in case of collision we have n't a big, crazy crew to swarm up from below deck and cut off our only chance to escape. There will be just you and me, and we 'll go halves on any chance that we may have to use."

(We were not reckoning on our third passenger then.)

" How about storms? " I asked.

" Have to take our chances.   If we get into a gale, I don't know any reason why we could n't sail along with it; in fact, we would have to.   Of course we depend upon air-currents largely, but not entirely. We can tack with our fins and machinery better than the average sailing-vessel can. But you will see all these things demon- strated.   A demonstration beats a diction- ary any day for fixing an idea."

We were ready on schedule time next morning.   Our supply of food and water was stowed away in a bulkhead aft, and the buzzing machine—the generator— occupied a similar bulkhead in the fore- castle.   I use the words " fore " and " aft," because it seems natural for a boat to have a stem and a stern; but the *Cloud Queen* might have had two afts and two fores, or vice versa, for I was never able to discover any difference in either end.   She was built on the same principle as a crab— either way was forward or backward, and nobody knew from her looks which way she was going. There was a sort of hold under our feet, as I have said; and in this the motor and batteries and all mechanisms were packed away as compactly as the works in a watch. These operated by switches and buttons arranged on a switch-board or sort of keyboard in front of Hill, who sat where the rudder ought to have been.

" I have been to a great deal of trouble," he said, " to get my engineering depart-ment ranged along small space like this, and it 's all on your account. I had but-tons here and there, like buttons on a coat, wherever they were needed, and switches hung up like birch rods in a school-room; but I knew if I got any one else in the boat we might be inadvertently touching three or four of them at once, and trying to do as many things all at the same time. Efforts of that nature would have led to endless complications, so I concluded to be on the safe side anyhow."

All the townspeople—in fact, every one who ever lived in that vicinity, except the dead and the bedridden and those who had emigrated to Canada (the United States are not so markedly French-colonial as Canada)—were on hand to see us off. We were ready to cast the last stay-lines loose, and the *Cloud Queen* was struggling and pulling to free herself, as if eager to set forth for her kingdom, when I happened to think of Jabez, my dog. Now Jabez was not a valuable animal in the kennel sense of the word. He had no pedigree, no sire of high degree with a string of blue ribbons over his oak entitling him to respect in the canine world. If he ever had a grandfather of any degree, Jabez never suspected it. Judging from his appearance, his family connections were good, but mixed. It would have puzzled an expert to tell what breed he belonged to, he seemed to be heir to so many races. To sum him up briefly, Jabez was just plain dog; but he was smart—so smart that I had found myself forced at times in his presence to spell words I did not wish him to understand, as one does with a child who exhibits signs of too much precocity.   He had cost me considerable, first and last, taking him around the country with me, and, looked at in that way, he was valuable.   I had paid fifty cents for him in the beginning, and every one considered that extortion.   After adding dog-tax yearly for ten years, bribing him out of the pound several times, and offering four rewards of five dollars each on the four separate occasions when he lost himself, to say nothing of having fed and clothed him, and bought dog patent medicine when required, I regarded him as a valuable animal; and as he grew in commercial value I found myself more and more unable to break off the attachment existing between us.   So I now bethought myself of my most faithful friend, and shouted to the innkeeper to look after him until my return.   But that worthy was shouting at us with equal energy: " Monsieur Hill, Monsieur Hill!   *Une momente —une momente!* "   He rushed into the house, and the next moment appeared with what seemed to be a bottle in his hand. Kind soul!  he was going to ask us to drink his health in the clouds. But an unexpected diversion occurred. There was a short bark, a flying leap, and Jabez landed in the boat. I had neglected to spell my instructions.

"Cast off! cast off!" shouted Hill, looking anxiously up. I reached my arm over the edge, and by making an effort—we sat so low in the body of the boat that only our heads were visible to any one on a level with us—leaned over to take the bottle. The next instant we shot up, amid cheers and shouts of laughter. Looking down, with my chin on the taffrail, I discovered the innkeeper's uplifted face, with an unmistakable expression of triumph on it as he regarded us. His head was cocked to one side, and there was a distinctly artistic glitter in his eye, which seemed to be focused appreciatively upon one particular spot. There was a brush in one hand and a paste-pot in the other. He had put a hotel paster on the *Cloud Queen*.

Our first sensation was similar to that one can experience any day by going downtown in New York and taking passage on

"A HOTEL PASTER ON THE 'CLOUD QUEEN.'"

the elevator in one of the new sky-scrapers there. The salvos of applause from beneath grew fainter and fainter. Jabez barked excitedly, and as Hill and I rose and leaned over the sides of the craft, he jumped and leaped in his efforts to lean over too.

"Jabez," I said, "you don't know it now, and you probably would not know it then, but if you jump overboard at this point you are booked to land right in eternity, with no accompanying funeral." I restrained him with one hand, while I waved a handkerchief with the other.

The scene we now looked upon was a curious one. The people we had left a moment before grew smaller and smaller; the upturned faces shrunk to the size of daisies in a field—of the petals of a daisy—of nothing. Like Chinamen after misdemeanors, they had all "lost their faces." We saw insects crawling around that were presumably horses and cattle. Roofs began to look like chips, and presently the whole town bunched together until it resembled a little pile of pebbles. By using our field-glasses we could discern what appeared to be a colony of very small two-legged ants running excitedly around in the yard we had left.

"They 've lost the leg of that last beetle," said Hill, with a grin.  "Now let us look at something bigger."

I cannot convey to you any adequate idea of my sensations when, for the first time, I beheld the wrinkled old face of the earth.  We use the term "the face of nature" ill-advisedly.  Now and then from some mountain-top we get a glimpse of an eyebrow, or a corner of the chin, or a bit of cheek; but at the best these glimpses are only fragmentary exhibitions of epidermis.  We never see the face of anything, any more than a fly crawling over a printed page sees anything but the individual letters as he travels over them one by one. But when you begin to get a perspective on the earth, when you get a mile or so away, then things change.  The dominant race of it begins to look the least of it. We saw here and there long, dark streaks crawling over the glaciers like caterpillars

—the herds of the valley of Chamonix being driven across the Montanvert and the Mer de Glace to summer pasturage on the mountains beyond.

" Imagine," said Hill, " that yonder lean herds are the troops of the first Napoleon, and think that all Europe marveled at such a feat.  It does not look much of a trick at this height, does it?  And think, too, up here, that a midge of a man made all Europe quake as well as marvel!  Warfare looks pretty small now, eh?  About as serious as a shadow gliding over a field of rye.  And you could not tell a Hannibal or Napoleon from a Sam Smith or John Jones from here, if you had them ranged up side by side.  It all depends on the point of view.  Things you look up to seem a great deal bigger and more difficult than the things you look down at—no difference whether it 's the Alps or an object of ambition.  You have to readjust your ideas as well as your glasses to make them fit distance.  For instance, look at the valley we slept in last night.  You see there are other little piles of pebbles here and there that we know are other towns. And there is a little white thread tangled around them—about number sixty, from its looks. That is the river Arva. And now you see the whole valley is only a faint wrinkle in the great face we are looking at. If the inhabitants were slaying each other in battle at this moment, and all the air ached with the sounds of anguish and was thick with the smell of blood, we should n't know it. Get away from the rip and roar of bullets, and all the world 's at peace."

The balloon, in close trim, had risen rapidly through the denser atmosphere near the earth, and now, in the higher altitude of lighter air, was going easier. We had exchanged summer heat for a brisk autumn-day temperature, with a touch of frost tempering the sunshine. The instrument for recording altitudes registered nine thousand feet.

" The only kind of warfare," appended Hill, holding down a button and heating a small disk from which we lighted cigars, " that we could appreciate here would be to see two or three thousand balloons lined up in battle array, shooting fire and profanity at each other, and calling bad names. That would be worth seeing. The fellow who could n't make his balloon dodge the shot he saw coming through the air would be pretty apt to see it shrivel up over his craft, and to take a header himself into the nearest landscape. Men will have to get into the air to fight their battles before long. They will have land and water bristling with guns so big that no one will dare to go to war in the twentieth century. Then, as man will never agree with man on all subjects, he will have to adjust his differences in the only available territory at hand, which will be the air. I consider the *Cloud Queen* to be the forerunner of those battle-ships."

As if pleased with the contemplation of some mental picture, he lapsed into silence, and began scanning the surrounding peaks with careful attention. I, too, had my glasses trained on those fair islands of the sky. They rose about us out of the air as the hill islands around Hong-Kong or

Rio de Janeiro rise out of the water—submerged mountain-peaks cast down, perhaps, from regions of eternal snows by some unrecorded quaking of the earth ages ago.   Jabez was at first under the impression that our field-glasses were some sort of double-barreled modern guns with which he was unfamiliar but willing to accept on evidence.   He looked and listened eagerly for game, or something to justify such unnecessarily long aims; but as no explosion followed, he concluded the invention was a failure, and devoted himself to the suppression of insurrection in his flea colony. Hill twisted around on his bench until he succeeded in getting his glasses trained on what he wanted, and then he consulted various compasses and instruments that were under glass before him.   He was as silent as a fog for a few minutes, but presently he said:

"Did you ever see a fish swim?"

"A few," said I.

"Well, then, you know that he fans himself along in the water, and steers with his tail and his spinal column.   If I could

"TO TAKE A HEADER INTO THE NEAREST LANDSCAPE."

make a craft on the principle of these jointed wooden snakes. you find in toy-shops, I could use fins precisely as a fish does; but as that did not seem practicable, I did the next best thing, and rigged up the boat with two tails. Between the boat and the two of them we have a limited sort of backbone, but it 's better than a splint, as you might say. I want to go over to that mountain, for instance,"—he pointed to one on the starboard side,—" and in order to do it we will set the fins going."

This being done, I was both amazed and amused to see that the action of the two fans at the ends of the boat was not unlike the movements of a fish's head and tail, while the side-fins, acting as paddles, fanned together, or on one side alone, according as Hill moved the switches before him. I could see without consulting the instruments that our course was changed, for our aërial landmarks came round before us as the shore does before a ship entering a harbor. Presently Hill said:

" Now I am going to give you an exhibition of the *Cloud Queen's* ability to descend at my will, without loss of gas. You know, most balloons carry sand-bags for ballast, and when they want to ascend they throw these bags out. Also, they can only come down by allowing gas to escape. That is a waste of floating energy that has been altogether obviated by an invention of mine. The generator with which we aided the manufacture of our motive power is capable of performing a variety of functions by different adjustments of the machinery. For instance, a full reversal produces an exactly opposite force from that you saw at work. I can make this reversal of energy more intelligible to you by likening it to a suction-pump; for the generator displaces the atmospheric air by which we are surrounded by sucking it up, thereby creating a decreased pressure beneath us, a sort of vacuum into which we naturally sink. Now,"—here he moved a switch, and there was a succession of sharp clicks below,—"if you could look overboard you would see that I have lowered some false sides to the boat that you had noticed below the fins, and these, fitting together in telescopic fashion, form a funnel. If you were outside you would perceive that the top of each panel is biforated with transverse slits, through which the atmospheric air escapes after it is drawn into the funnel by the pump. Mind not to hang a hand inadvertently over the edge while we go down. I explain this at length beforehand, because the process is rather noisy—so much so, in fact, that it renders conversation difficult."

"Rather noisy!" The next minute we were in the midst of a revelry of chaotic sound, beside which the noise made by the generator in the hotel courtyard was as the gentle sighings of May zephyrs compared with the roar of a cyclone. Talk about conversation being difficult! We could not have heard a steamer's fog-horn two rods away; and the worst of it was that the noise was of such an awful nature. In addition to the thud and whir of what might have been a steam-yacht's pistons displaced under our feet, the vibration of which made the flesh shake on our bones, there was a most demoniac whistling going on around our edges. The atmosphere escaped through those biforated panels with yells and shrieks of agony. A gale whistling and shrilling through cordage is an uncanny sound to hear, but that assailing our ears was indescribable. I could only liken it to several hundred big steam-whistles and sirens being let off together a few feet away. The combination was something appalling, and it would not have surprised me to see the stars rattling out of heaven. Jabez scratched frantically at the bottom of the boat, where his deadliest enemy seemed to be located; then tried to put his paws over his ears; and at last, in desperation, sprang into my lap and jammed his head under my arm. A moment after he wriggled down, pointed his nose heavenward, and shut his eyes. I knew from the workings of his countenance that he believed himself to be howling. His nose bubbled with his efforts and anxiety; but with his head between my knees I was aware that he was making no more noise than a water-lily. Now and then he opened his eyes, and I saw in them an expression of surprised inquiry. He was going through all the howling formula, but where was the howl? I pitied him, for I knew that Jabez was as badly off as the man who was too deaf to hear himself think.

Hill took an envelop out of his pocket, tore it up, and tossed the pieces overboard. They whisked up out of sight so fast that our eyes could hardly follow them. He nodded in a satisfied way, got out his glasses again, and looked at his instruments. Then he threw the switch back, and the noise ceased as suddenly as it had begun. Jabez heard his own howl, and seemed pleased with it, for he repeated it. Then he writhed around on his back and tried to scratch what was left of the noise out of his ear.

"How was that?" asked Hill. "We came down at the rate of about five hundred feet per second."

"It 's not bad for speed," said I; "but for noise it beats anything I ever heard. Have we got to do that again in order to get back to terra firma?"

"NO MORE NOISE THAN A WATER-LILY."

" Perhaps.   Why ? "

" Because," said I, with feeling, " I think Jabez and I will take the quieter route overboard instead.   Talk about modern guns!   They 're not in it; I would sooner take the chances of cracking my ear-drums on a man-of-war in action than trust to the voice of the generator."   Jabez was trying his hearing by twisting his head from side to side and shaking it violently at intervals.   He thought the trouble had all been in his ears.

" Yes," said Hill; " it does make an awful row.   I 've always contended that we hear too much in this noisy old world. We are obliged to notice sounds with which we have no concern, but that nevertheless distract us, and prevent the best and most effective concentration of faculty.   But you see, with our atmosphere, things crash together like cymbals. A wheel smites a pavement; a foot acts on the earth like a blow on a sounding-board.   And then, think of the hammers, and what effect they have on the air and, through it, on our ears!   On the other hand, did you ever think what a lot of things we do not hear? Our senses are too dull to catch the little fine chorus underground where the roots work. We hear the leaves rustle, and we know that the corn sings, and the tall grass. Under proper conditions of development we ought to hear the flowers bloom. I have no doubt but that there are solos and choruses and psalms in the gardens and fields that are not produced by birds. If the morning stars sang together, why should not the roses sing as they blossom? We are mostly undeveloped—for the higher harmonies anyhow. Why, look at that dog. What his tongue lacks his nose gains. He has three senses where we have two. Does he accept the evidence of his eyes alone, or of his eyes and ears together? Not he! He says, 'Now, nose, you umpire this game. Eyes say so and so; ears say so and so. Which is it?' He does n't know much, but he knows better than to trust to one faculty alone, as we do when we say, 'Seeing is believing'; don't you, Jabez?"

Jabez wagged assent, and lolled at the compliment.

"Now," continued my curious friend, "to come back to practical things, we have taken a tack in altitude in order to give you a chance to see a celebrated spot on the map." He rose to his feet, placed his hands trumpet-fashion around his mouth in true seaman style, and shouted through them:

"Hospice, ahoy!"

This astonishing performance in mid-air struck me as being much more curious than it really was; for I did not then realize that we were capable of traversing space in our craft at a much faster rate than the average train of cars. I looked over the side of the boat, and beheld the walls of the great St. Bernard. But I had no sooner seen them than they were blotted from my view as if by utter annihilation. A cloud had suddenly swept down and enveloped us like a blanket. Through this we could hear surprised voices questioning one another. I translate as nearly as I may from memory.

"Heardest thou the voice? There must be some one coming up the pass."

"Nay; were the pass above us, that might be, but the voice I heard came from the clouds."

"Holy Mother! thus I thought also; but what think you it can be?"

"I know not; but listen—perhaps it may come again."

Hill looked at me through the mist, and nodded; then again he hailed. There was a hurried consultation, a scurrying of sandals on the stones, and then a different voice, one with authority and an accent of culture—the abbot's, probably:

"Loose the dogs. If it be as thou say'st, a traveler climbing the mountain may lose his way, and perish by falling from a height."

Now, whether it was the sound of the word "dogs," which Jabez knew the meaning of as well as I did, or the unusual aspect of things, or what, I do not know, but at this moment our canine companion fell to barking with might and main. At this all the big dogs in the convent kennels responded, and there rose about us a chorus of deep " Woof, woof, woofs!" led by Jabez in high tenor. This continued for several minutes, and during that time it would have been impossible for any one to locate a sound with any degree of certainty. In the midst of it the cloud lifted as swiftly as it had swept down upon us, disclosing to view the convent yards and roofs. All the brothers save one had departed upon their business; and this one, as Hill hailed him again, gave us a frightened look, crossed himself, and retreated hastily to summon his superior. The dogs stood their ground, and expressed their opinion of this apparition out of the clouds in no half-hearted manner.

"Who are you?" said one, in what Jabez evidently took to be a supercilious manner, for he resented it.

" A self-respecting, gentledog, sir, and good as you are any day, sir."

"Woof!" said the big dog; "I 'll wager you would n't know a paternoster from a pancake!" I could see Jabez fairly wink with indignation at this.

"You show me a pancake, and I 'll show you whether I do or not," said he. The big dog started to retort in scornful fashion, but was interrupted by another convent dog of gentler manners and more Christian disposition.

"Do you want to be rescued?" this one inquired kindly.

"Not that I know of, just now, thank you," said Jabez, mollified at once.

"Because if you do, I was just wondering how we were going to manage it," said the second dog. "I have had some experience getting people out of the snow in winter, but I never hauled a rescue in from the air."

The conversation was interrupted here by the appearance of the abbot, followed by the lay brother who had first discovered us. He was a simple fellow evidently, for he crossed himself, and blinked apprehensively at us. Other monks came dribbling out of doors here and there, each filled with wonder and curiosity. The abbot greeted us very cordially.

"Welcome, messieurs!" he exclaimed;

"welcome!   Will you not descend?   Do you come from Paris?   Ah,"—not waiting for an answer to any of his questions,—" I trust you have solved the problem of aëronautics!   Not since the siege of '70 have I seen a balloon.   I was in Paris then.   I saw Gambetta depart by balloon for Tours.   Ah, what a sight!   What enthusiasm—*mon Dieu!*   Messieurs are French, perhaps?"

"Next door to it," answered Hill; "Americans."

"*Oui, oui,*" said the abbot, waving his hand politely; "the greatest nation in the world.   Its enterprise, its growth"—he made a comprehensive gesture with both arms—"marvelous!   *Oui,* monsieur; nothing short of marvelous.   America first, France second, among all the nations of the world in progress and enlightenment."

"Reverse the positions, reverend father," said Hill, not to be outdone in politeness, "and then we shall agree."

But the abbot shook his head vigorously, and protested.   It was as if he said,

"What! a Frenchman, well born, and impolite to his guests? Monstrous! not to be thought of!"

After a little further conversation of equal unimportance, we departed with the benedictions of all the brotherhood ringing in our ears, and a tremendous expression from the dogs, that we took to be the assurance of good wishes and *bon voyage* at least.

". I suppose it did n't occur to you to wonder how we hung motionless in the air like that for so long a time," remarked Hill, as we sailed away.

"No," said I; "it did not. If I stopped to marvel at all the wonderful things you do with this machine, I should spend my days at it."

"Well," said Hill, "I threw out an electric anchor, or a grappling-iron—that 's the best term for it. Our electricity was holding on to a boulder just outside the convent walls. Otherwise we should not have had so much time to visit."

"Oh," said I, "I 'm getting calloused to marvels, keeping company with them right along.   I look upon the whole machine as a miracle anyhow.   You could n't surprise me if you tried."

But I spoke airily and without foundation for my remarks.   I was to be very much surprised before we were through with that excursion.

After leaving the convent we ascended very rapidly, and it was getting colder and colder.   Our breaths began to be visible, and we donned top-coats, but still we were chilled.   As we arose we took note of the phenomena which puzzle balloonists.   We saw the earth beneath us arched like a reversed sky — a great gulf of air, deepest in the middle, and with cliff-like shores of Alpine ranges.   Instead of the convex curve one would expect to see, sloping away on the sides and highest in the middle, following the supposed curve of the earth, we saw the land beneath us hollowed like a saucer, with a rim rising heavenward, just as the inverted arch of the sky appears to fit over the world like a lid when one looks up.   We were in the sky, but a strange sky of intense Prussian blue. Clouds formed below us, the evaporization taking place from snow-peaks warming under the sun; but above and around us was that deep, uncanny sea of metallic blue, marvelous in its luminous depth.

"There are various causes assigned for this effect," said Hill. "Some scientists claim that the reflection from vesicles of water occasions this change of color. Now I differ. The polarizing angle of the air is forty-five degrees. It is impossible that there should be moisture at this height. Ascending particles have long since frozen and fallen in the form of snow upon the mountains. We have got to consider air as a soluble fluid—that is, the atmosphere; and we must also take into consideration the fact that up here we get a perspective on it, and it is bluer than the deep sea. On the surface of the earth it seems thin and impalpable, and we cannot look at it —there is nothing to see. But it is dense in large quantities, and, like a glass of sea-water, it does not look blue in the glass. Here 's another curious thing, too," he went on.   " Have you noticed that, except when we had the fins going, or the suction-pump,—in one case we were cutting across currents, and in the other through them, —it has been impossible to determine whether we were going fast or slow, or, for the matter of that, whether we were going at all?   That is the beauty of being carried by the air.   There is no friction, and to all appearances the balloon may be as motionless as Mohammed's coffin, when in fact it is covering space at the rate of a mile a minute."

Presently, having consulted various clocks and watches and instruments, he said:

" We are now fifteen thousand feet above sea-level, and that "—he made a gesture like a showman exhibiting his chief attraction—" that is Mont Blanc."

I looked in the direction indicated, and saw what might have been an island in the sea—a strange, chalky island rising out of a blue ocean, on which were curious waves —round, white, petrified waves, or semi-petrified, at any rate—moving sluggishly, like half-cooled lava. The sun shone on their woolly crests, and on the great dome of the mountain, until it and they glittered as if powdered with diamond-dust. There was an unreal, theatrical glamour about the whole scene that was fascinating in the extreme when one considered that what seemed so unreal was the crowning reality of Europe. Hill trained his glass on the mountain, and then made some calculations with his pencil. Presently he said:

"That reminds me, it 's time for lunch —past time by two hours. Why did n't you say so?"

I took stock of my sensations, and concluded that I had been too much excited to realize that I was hungry. Now that the subject was mentioned, I felt a certain deficiency in the program, not taken note of before; so we ate, with the approval and assistance of Jabez, and Hill formulated his plans for the day.

"You see," said he, "I want to make our maximum ascent to-day. In the first place, the gas is in prime condition; in the next place, if we waited until to-morrow we should find that the balloon would fall perceptibly, owing to the action of the sun's heat after a night of cold. Being extremely sensitive, it would at once commence to radiate heat into space, cooling itself rapidly by that process, and becoming heavier. Naturally it would descend. Now I have never before attempted going up in proximity to snow-mountains, and I am not positive what the effect will be upon the ascension properties of the *Cloud Queen.* I know we can do it all right now, and we still have time enough and to spare before we lose the sun. What do you say? Shall we try it?"

"By all means," said I.

"Then prepare," replied Hill, "to be carried farther away from the earth than any mortal has ever been before. There is a record of thirty-seven thousand feet —seven miles—made by Glashier and Coxwell, that I am going to break. It 's time to get out our bunting, old man." He proceeded with great gravity to stick a small silken flag in a socket at one end, and the *Cloud Queen* unfurled the stars

"THE BEST OF FLAGS ON EARTH."

and stripes. "That," said Hill, regarding it affectionately, "is a sight for men and angels. Here's to it! We are going to smash the record, or something, all for the glory of the United States of America. Come, now, with a will—hip, hip, hurrah! Hurrah for the best country, and the best flag, and the best balloon on earth!"

We gave it with a will, assisted by Jabez, who was patriotic to the core, and independent even in the clouds; and then we settled back comfortably with our pipes, while the *Cloud Queen* rose majestically toward skies unknown.

# II

THE milky island over our starboard side seemed to sink gradually. We first lost sight of the cotton-wool waves around its cliffs, then the chalk cliffs themselves, then the snowy summits. There was nothing but the sun and the *Cloud Queen* left in space.

Jabez was still cheering for the United States. He gathered in his breath to the point of explosion, and discharged volley after volley of barks at the flag, at the balloon overhead, at salient points in his own recollection of things he had not had time to do real justice to before. The rebound from each volley cast him back against the sides of the craft like a muzzle-loading gun overcharged with powder, and presently, having barked at everything in sight and several invisible subjects, he sat down lolling, and searched the horizon for some new topic.

"It is possible," said Hill, removing his pipe for a moment, "that we may be rather uncomfortable up there. Glashier experienced a semi-paralysis at the height of five and a half miles, and lost consciousness altogether at six. Coxwell suffered from cold, but retained the possession of his faculties sufficiently to pull the valve-rope and release gas enough to lower them into a warmer temperature, where both revived. Now in case I should lose my head or become incapable of directing the *Cloud Queen*, and you find that you also experience warning sensations, try to remember this: the third switch, marked 'No. 3,' sets the suction-pump at work, and that would pull us down without loss of gas. Don't touch the valve-rope except as a last resort, for I shall have to release the pressure very materially within the next few minutes in order to prevent our being torn to pieces by the gas inside. You see, as the external air becomes lighter and its pressure decreases, the expansive force of the confined gas becomes proportionately greater. That is the chief danger we have to fear at this height—unless we should both become unconscious and freeze to death."

Neither prospect was attractive. Hill replaced his pipe, fumbled around under the seat, and drew out two thick Scotch blankets. He handed one to me, wrapped the other around himself, and turned up his collar. Then he threw a switch on the board before him, and I heard the paddle-wheel begin to whir-r-r in the balloon above us.

"It *is* getting cold," said he, looking at his thermometer as if to assure himself that such a conclusion was justifiable. Cold! it was cold enough to freeze the fleas on Jabez. We smoked our pipes out, and presently fell to slapping our sides with our hands, as coachmen do on winter days when the frost bites. Jabez liked it at first, but as it grew colder and colder he realized the futility of trying to get out a winter coat on such short notice, and took refuge under the blanket.

" Feel queer ? " asked Hill.

I consulted my feelings, and replied in the negative.

" Well, I should n't wonder if we stood it pretty comfortably. You see, we 've been cruising around in high altitudes all day and getting used to rarefied air. It 's as easy to get used to as a rare beefsteak; all you want is a little practice—though I have felt pretty sick myself practising, and at that time I saw a man die on the mountains in South America. We had gone up that infernal little railroad from Lima to Chicla—ever been there? Well, passengers who fail to stop on the way up and get used to short rations of air find it pretty hard foraging at the top. You feel just like a fish out of water—gasping for breath, and no breath to be had at any price. It 's an awful sensation; it 's drowning in the air. I 've never had any use for angling since then: I know too well how the fish feels when he drowns out of water."

The sky around us grew bluer and bluer, and even the sun had long since ceased to appear natural. It was a great deal easier sitting still than making any effort, but I crawled over to the edge, rested my chin on the taffrail, and looked down. The mountains lay in corrugated ridges under us, streaked with infinitesimal chasms lying like hair-lines on the surface. Everything

"TRYING TO CORRUPT A TEMPERANCE DOG."

had shrunken, and objects on the earth might have been at the small end of a telescope.

"I think it is time," said Hill, "to put on a little fuel." He took a flask out of his pocket, poured some of its contents into a glass, and handed it to me. It was good old brandy, and it tingled my blood into warmth. I offered some to Jabez, who was shivering, and looking as if he would like to know when the next train left for Chamonix; but he reproached me with his eyes for trying to corrupt a temperance dog who was six miles away from home.

"Now," said Hill, "unsling your glasses and make the most of time. You will probably never have another chance like this to look at the pygmean world. There is the republic of France; and there is the domain of the little king—though all domains look little at this height, and all kings' look not at all. Now come over to this side. There is Humbert's territory— Humbert's and the Pope's. And now look over in that direction—over Kaiserward. Do you see that little slab of country just over that farther hummock of ground? That 's Alsace-Lorraine; there have been more scraps over that territory than over a contest for mayor of Mudville. Would you give Jabez for the whole of it, up here? Off in those dim distances lie Germany and England. The Turk is busy kicking up shines just over in the other direction, and past that little blot of deep blue—like an overturned ink-bottle—Africa lies beyond the Mediterranean. I wish we had a Lick telescope. Great guns of Washington! I *wish* we could get high enough to see America."

Of course I echoed the sentiment. We had been annoyed by the constant necessity of clearing the fog of our breaths from the lenses, and now, lowering my glass a moment for that purpose, I was startled when I glanced at Hill. His nose was quite white. For a moment I thought he was feeling the effects of the high air, but the next minute I realized that it was cold instead.

"Great Scott!" I exclaimed, "your nose is frozen." He put his hand up to his face with a start, and looked at me.

"So is yours," he said. It was true. We abandoned our survey of Europe and devoted our attention to ourselves. I thought of the Alps down below.

"No wonder the earth freezes her noses poking them up into the air like this."

But Hill interrupted me with a yell that brought Jabez out from under the blanket like a catapult shot, and even made me jump. Our aëronaut was dancing around the boat until it rocked.

"We 're up forty-three thousand feet!" he declaimed. "Good for America! Good for the greatest country on earth!" (It was noticeable that as European nations diminished in size the value of America invariably grew in importance.) Hill dropped into his seat with a thud, and gazed at the register with admiration. "That beats the Dutch!" he exclaimed presently in an awe-struck tone. He looked at me, at the balloon, at Jabez, and back again to his instruments. But pretty soon his face clouded. He again looked at the balloon—anxiously this time. I looked too, but could see nothing unusual. Hill clutched his instrument and bent over it.

"According to this infernal machine, we are descending at the rate of a mile a minute," he said.

"I don't believe it," said I.

"I hope you 're right," he answered,

"but I observe we no longer hear the paddle-wheel revolve, and I should like to
know when in Sam Patch it stopped—and
me not know it!"

The metaphor of this remark was mixed,
but the facts were plain enough. I became
aware that an ominous silence reigned
where the whir of the wheel had previously
sounded, and I also knew that we both had
been so excited that neither one of us
could say when it had actually stopped.
It might have been two or three minutes
before; at any rate, it had stopped. I
looked overboard. Mont Blanc was rising
beneath us, and I felt justified in respecting
the conclusions of the machine on the
dropping question.

They say that when a man is drowning
he reviews all the scenes in his past life in
a few seconds, crowding the events of the
long, slow years together into the moment
or two he believes he has left, and that he
thinks with wonderful clearness. I have
no doubt whatever but that in the two or
three minutes that followed while we sat
waiting for the crash we both did the

same, though I am bound to testify for Hill that, whatever his thoughts were, there was no trace of anxiety or apprehension on his countenance. His eyes were fixed upon his instruments, and the two or three remarks he made were in his ordinary tone. As for myself, I had been so recently above the clouds, I had seen the old civilized world reduced to such a pygmy by distance, I had been so imbued by the thought of the littleness of the biggest greatness, that I appeared to myself too much of an atom to take serious account of. I felt no terror; rather a quickened interest—a wonder if the end of all things to me as a unit of the human universe would come in the next few minutes.

"I hope the instruments won't be smashed," said Hill, with great earnestness. "Confound it! I wish I could be sure. If we can only drop somewhere in the track of mountain-climbers, or a herder, or somebody—*any*body to find these reports and take them back! They would be of the greatest possible interest to science." He had been scribbling busily in a little book, and this he now slipped under a projection of the keyboard before him. "Is n't it strange," he added, "that the frailest things, like feathers or pieces of paper, survive a fall of three or four miles without injury, while flesh and blood, or metal even, are not to be found?" He sighed profoundly, but I knew the sigh was not for himself, but rather for his records.

It was impossible for me to tell whether we were descending at the terrific rate registered. So far, after the first sensation of upward flight, after getting away from sliding things by which to reckon like a Chinaman's slate, we might have been motionless, for all I knew. The temperature had grown suddenly warmer, as I knew from the way my nose ached. It felt as chilled fingers or toes do when brought suddenly into the warmth of a room, and I could see by the way Hill nursed his that the prospect of immediate eternity had not altogether distracted his attention from the ache in anatomy. Presently he said very quietly:

"There! we 've struck the aërial gulf

stream.    I guess we are safe enough now. We are not going down anything like so fast."

This was true enough, but we were sinking into night.   We had long since got out of range of the sun, and as the gray old earth rolled over in its airy bed it grew darker and darker under its own shadow. I could see that Hill was straining his eyes, and as I looked out I caught a glimpse of Mont Blanc near at hand—Mont Blanc only a stone's throw away, grim and ghostly in the darkness as the specter of the Brocken.   Then I was suddenly aware of little, fine, granular bits of snow falling on my face and hands.   In a few seconds we were in the midst of great white flakes whirling about us like big feathers, and all view of mountains, or anything at hand save these noiseless companions, was blotted from sight.   Hill was fumbling around with his switches and buttons, but without avail.   There appeared to be no response from any of them, if I might judge from the absolute silence into which we sank deeper and deeper.

"Why don't you fire off your light-gun?" I asked.

"The confounded thing does n't work, or I would have done so long ago. That 's the trouble with electricity: it 's as liable to go back on you as a fickle girl."

He scratched a match, and in that brief moment of illumination we were able to distinguish nothing but softly falling flakes against a blank wall of impenetrable darkness. Its light also shone upon Hill's face anxiously inspecting his instruments, and upon the snowflakes like a swarm of ghostly bees in the background.

"We are falling very gently," said he, presently; "but I should like to know why we have n't hit something. With Mont Blanc as near as it looked, we should have struck terra firma five minutes ago. We must be drifting away in this cloud." But even as he spoke the snow ceased, or we passed out of the belt of it. At the same moment we were aware that the *Cloud Queen* had met with some obstruction. She was grounding somewhere, but, curiously enough, the top part, or balloon proper, was grounding first. We had not felt a jar or vibration in the craft in which we sat, but there were raking sounds overhead, and bits of snow and ice fell upon us. Jabez regarded these as assaults from unseen enemies, and resented them accordingly. There was a peculiar property to the sound of his barking now, as if it came back from a wall. We were sure that we were on the mountain-side. At no time had the sounds of contact above been sufficient to arouse alarm, and now they altogether ceased. Everything was silent again for a minute or two, and then we felt the *Cloud Queen* ground in reality on the bottom. There were two or three soft bumps, a lurch or two, and everything was quiet.

"I had a tallowed wick here somewhere," said Hill, lighting another match and hunting around for it. "Wait until I find it, and we will soon see where we are, to say nothing about getting the light-gun in order."

When the wick finally flared up I saw a glittering wall of ice, sheer as a house, at my right. There was another wall of blue ice at the left, and high as we could see at both sides these icy cliffs extended. Forward and back of us there seemed to be caverns stretching away, and a great pile of soft snow, or what appeared to be new-

"HILL CLAMBERED OUT OF THE BOAT."

fallen snow, lay just ahead. There was evidently some sort of projecting eave over us, and we had come down the side that was not impeded by that roof or eave. Perhaps its protruding edges were what the *Cloud Queen* had brushed on her way past. Hill clambered out of the boat in

silence, taking the wick with him.  Jabez
followed, sniffing curiously at everything
he passed; and I stretched my stiff legs,
while man and dog went down the gorge
together, casting long shadows behind, but
striking off innumerable sparks as the light
of the taper was caught by and reflected
from hundreds of glittering projections and
irregularities in the icy walls.  They went
only a little way, and then Hill returned
and stood beside me.

"Well, I 'll be hanged!" he exclaimed.
"Where do you suppose we are?"

"Give it up."

He looked at me reflectively, and then
at the ball of wick in his hand.

"As near as I can make out," he said,
"by the aid of this lightning-bug of a
lamp, we are at the very bottom of the
very deepest crevasse in all Mont Blanc."

I suppose I looked blank myself; at any
rate, the sight of my face set him off.  He
leaned against the ice behind him, and
laughed until the taper flickered and shook
in his grasp.

"Talk about ballooning!" he exclaimed

when he had recovered his equanimity. "When I invited you to go into the air with me, you did not expect my invitation

"LEANED AGAINST THE ICE AND LAUGHED."

also included side-trips into the earth and down wells, did you? I don't wonder you look dazed; but just hold the light, man, while I gear up the machinery a bit. I don't know how it is with you, but what *I* want is tea."

He set to work cheerfully, and presently the fumes of a good supper arose appetizingly as if served from Delmonico's kitchen. The electric current once in order, he also gave me an exhibition of the light-gun's powers that seemed nothing short of magical. That singular invention defied all known laws for the transmission of light, and I could see what a terrible illuminating-engine it might become in the hands of an enemy, in a balloon, for instance, inspecting at his leisure the fortifications beneath him. By a combination of the lenses, the workings of which he never explained to me, he could throw ahead what appeared to be globes of light, detached from the light in the gun, to all appearances, and yet illuminating like lamps as they passed through the air or remained motionless, suspended against or over anything he wished specially to inspect. The effect of these luminous and, to all appearances, independent bodies of light was weird and ghostly in the extreme, and I could imagine the consternation one of them would create in a fortress. To be sure, the life of a light-ball was only a few seconds if the operator wished to avoid any visible connection with it, but, as Hill said, that was "worlds for photographic purposes."

"I adjust the focus," said he, "at a hundred feet, we will say. Then, by an arrangement of the refracting crystals inside, I produce a round, concentrated globule of intense light, which is magnified from one to a thousand times by the lense according as I set it, and deposited, as you might say, upon the wall of darkness one hundred feet ahead of the muzzle of the light-gun. If one could get high enough in the rare and purified air to work direct with the luminiferous and cosmic ether, with a light-gun of sufficient power, it would be possible to produce moons—say a moon for each county, eh? 'No more oil-lamps or gas or arc-lights on street corners, but moons for everybody—every man his own moon-maker.'   How would that read for an ad.?"

" First-class," said I; " but how about clouds?"

Hill sighed profoundly.   " That 's the trouble," said he.   " We all know how clouds hoodoo a real, simon-pure, genuine moon product; and as artificial moons would have to be made above the cloud strata in order to take advantage of the ether with luminous possibilities—well, somebody has got to invent a process by which clouds can be dispelled first, before county moons can be put on the market. But I am more interested just now in the supper market."

I felt that I was, too; and as Jabez never yet preferred a moon to a beefsteak, we all agreed upon that subject, and ate our well-cooked meal in a palace whose like no Mogul king ever dined in.   And afterward we slept very comfortably in spite of our frost-bites, for the ice-cavern seemed warm by contrast with the cold we had suffered from in the sky.   Next morning I was awakened by the sound of hammering on metal directly over my ears, and opened my eyes to see Hill at work upon his crippled inventions.

"That is the rising-gong," said he, as I started up.

"Is it? It sounds to me more like Cramp's shipyard. I suppose it would be inappropriate to say 'The top av the morning to yez,' would n't it?"

"The top! It looks to me more like the bottom of everything—morning, day, mountain, the whole terrestrial business, in fact. Just cast your eyes up, my friend, and tell me how you think we ever got down here, and, what would be more to the point, how you think we are ever going to get out of here."

I looked up and saw a thin blue ribbon of sky no wider than a lady's belt—or so it seemed to my inexperienced eyes. Yet there lay the balloon, or reclined, rather, apparently full of gas, but altogether lacking buoyancy. It was half supported by the sides of the crevasse, and the ice-walls that had seemed so close together in the night were in reality far enough apart to admit a bag capable of carrying ninety thousand cubic feet of gas, although less than half this quantity had been actually used, as more would have been dangerous when making allowance for the expansion caused by outside air-currents of different temperatures.

"Do you remember asking me what was to hinder the gas from congealing in high altitudes?" asked Hill.

"Yes; and you said that you were going to paddle it around—to keep it churned up; and you also propounded a conundrum about the relative weights of ice and water."

"That 's right," said Hill; "there 's nothing the matter with your memory yet. Well, I 'm blessed if that congealing process is not precisely what has taken place. The minute the paddle stopped Jack Frost got to work. That bag might just as well be filled with ditch-water so far as any self-sustaining property goes." He took off his cap and rubbed his head, in thoughtful contemplation of the spectacle before him. "Look here," he added, giving the valve-rope a jerk. There was no hiss of escaping gas, no shrinkage of the enveloping fabric.

We were in a strange, green sort of twilight at the bottom of the crevasse, and the walls about us might have been glass, they were so clear and transparent. At the extreme top we could detect an overhanging, eave-like mass, beautifully curved and chiseled at the edges by the wind. After a while the sun shone upon it, and we concluded that it was the mountain-side of our roofless cavern, and that the opposite edge was possibly much lower. We also discovered that the crevasse was wider just there than anywhere else, curving at both sides like a round well. Into that well—the only spot in all the Alps probably where such an object as the *Cloud Queen* could have descended—it had been our luck to drop.

"Do you remember, a great many years ago," asked Hill, "seeing a schooner aground in Lincoln Park in just such a way as this? She had been driven ashore by a great storm that wrecked many similar craft, but it was her luck to be carried by the waves through the only spot along the whole lake front where there was no breakwater.  We have accomplished pretty much the same feat."

It did indeed appear so, and the *Cloud Queen* looked to me to be a great deal worse off than the schooner had been.

"You see that overhanging eave up there?" continued Hill.  "Do you know what that is?  That is destruction; that is the foot of a glacier.  It may not fall to-day, nor to-morrow; but when the time comes, and the sun warms and melts the accumulating mass behind sufficiently to loosen it from the rocks to which it is at present frozen, it will start upon its journey, and whoever is down here might much better be elsewhere.  A part of it will inevitably be swept over the fissure mouth above, carried by its own momentum; but a cataract of ice and snow will pour down —enough, perhaps, to fill this well up as though it had never been."

I must confess that this revelation shook my spirit more than the prospect of immediate destruction had the night before.

"Of course," added Hill, probably seeing me change color, " as I said, it may
not fall to-day, nor to-morrow, nor while
we are here. But that is just the point.
I have explored this fissure in both direc-
tions, and so far as I can see, our chances
to get out are about equal to a beetle's in
a glass jar. You see," — he smiled grimly,
— " it 's only one of those errors of human
judgment to which we all are liable. When
I started for the clouds I naturally did not
outfit for climbing; in fact, I could have
made only a limited provision for that sort
of expedition — like wings and gum shoes,
for instance, and you know the market for
wings is poor. But mountain-climbing —
that 's different. We need — and we lack
— ice-axes, nails in the soles of our shoes,
guides, ropes, experience, and a few other
important items. We 're about as well off
for mountain-climbing as we are for cloud-
climbing; and in the mean time there 's
the avalanche getting ready — packing up
to move."

"Well," said I, "we need not camp
right under this impending doom. We

can go farther down the cañon, as it were."

"That 's true; but, on the other hand, the balloon is our only visible means of escape, so far as I can see."

"You don't mean to say that you think the balloon, even if it could be made to float again, could get out of this circumscribed place without ripping itself to pieces?"

"She got down that way."

"To be sure; but look at those jagged sides. Some of those projections are like knife-blades."

"They were just as sharp last night," persisted Hill, doggedly.

"Yes; but suppose there were cuts in the bag; you would n't know it now. How can you find out with absolute certainty until the gas thaws?"

"I 've inspected the bag pretty thoroughly, and there is not a thread cut, to the best of my belief."

"I hope you 're right. If you are it simplifies our getting out of this predicament."

" Ah," said Hill, sighing and shaking his head, " there 's the rub!   Instead of simplifying our unfortunate position, it complicates it.   How long do you suppose it would take to thaw forty or fifty thousand cubic feet of congealed gas,—in an icehouse, at that,—and at what expenditure of electrical force?   Now my storage battery contains only enough power to refill the balloon once, with an allowance of enough amperes to keep the light-gun supplied with force, or the descending-pump, and to boil an occasional tea-kettle.   If I exhaust half the force thawing the congealed gas I shall have remaining only enough watts to half fill the balloon—which would not mean sufficient buoyancy to float it."

" Cheerful prospect," said I, sitting down on the edge of the boat.   " How many days did you say you provisioned for?"

" Six—not reckoning on Jabez.   His rations reduce it to about four.   However, we can only hope, like Mr. Micawber, that ' something will turn up.' "

"It would be more apt to turn down here."

"That 's right. But let us breakfast. Things won't look so gloomy on full stomachs."

I helped him to detach the chains from the balloon, and we dragged the boat far enough away to be, as we calculated, out of range of the avalanche when it should conclude to start on its trip. Then we cooked our breakfast and discussed the situation.

"Here 's another thing I did n't mention," said Hill. "You know what a confounded row the generator makes when at work, but you may not know that avalanches are sometimes started by sounds; the slightest vibration in the air may shake them off their perches when they are poised for falling. Why, in some Alpine villages the ringing of church bells is prohibited during the avalanche season; and I have heard experienced guides dilate upon the necessity for silence at some points on the mountains known to be particularly menaced by that sort of danger. Climbing

"DRAGGED THE BOAT OUT OF RANGE."

parties are cautioned to step lightly and to speak in whispers. Now if that glacier overhead is balancing for flight, how would the noise of the generator affect it, do you think?"

"Well," said I, "if the crack of a twig, or the sound of a human voice, a cough or a sneeze, or the ringing of one of those two-penny Alpine bells, can alarm a full-grown avalanche, I see no reason why the whole mountain should not slide off its base when you start the generator going."

"That's just about it," said Hill, resignedly.

We ate our breakfast, and started out to explore the ice-gorge to its end, hoping to find some means of egress. As nearly as we could determine by the compass,— which might be deflected by mineral deposits in the mountain, for all we knew,— the crevasse ran northwest by southeast from the spot where the balloon had fallen. In some places the ice-walls seemed to meet overhead, and in no place was there a wider opening at the top than that well-like hole over the *Cloud Queen*. We decided its length to be perhaps three quarters of a mile, or a mile; but this was only at the bottom. At the top it was bridged here and there, and doubtless appeared from above to be a number of deep crevasses rather than the one deep slit in the ice and rocks we had found it to be. At one end there was a narrow, perpendicular wall of rock that we could have climbed had it not overhung at the top like the branches of a tree. A monkey could not have escaped by it. At the northern end there were nothing but ice-walls, bare and smooth as glass. Irregular piles of ice and snow, varying in depth, and showing by their formation that they had poured down from above, lay here and there along the bottom of the fissure. This gave color and foundation to Hill's theory of what might be expected from that quarter, and we took great pains to drag the boat and its supplies to a place free from these indications and with no overhanging eaves. We discussed various plans, abandoning them all as impracticable and so the first day passed. It was a short day, for it grew dark very early down where we were, and the night was the longest I ever experienced. We did not sleep well, although we had nothing to fear from avalanches at night.

Jabez was the only one of the family who had a good time. He had nothing to worry about, and so maintained a cheerful spirit—as almost any one can in those circumstances. He amused himself with bits of ice or rock, growling and barking like a whole kennel full of dogs, even when I expostulated with him and told him he was liable to scare up an avalanche when he least expected or wanted it. When we organized exploring expeditions in the hope of finding some overlooked rift in the rock through which we might crawl to freedom, he pioneered ahead, stopping now and then to wave an encouraging tail, and to bark with undiminished ardor; but even his voice sounded unnatural down there. We imagined it had lost its tone of merry hope. Anything he said or we said sounded as sepulchral as saying " Boo!" in a barrel.

"AMUSED HIMSELF WITH BITS OF ICE."

We were at lunch on the second day when an unexpected diversion occurred. Something fell from above, striking the wall near by with a sharp clink. We both sprang to our feet, thinking this must be the forerunner of an avalanche.

" That 's singular," said Hill. " I 've heard ice tinkle, but I never heard it ring before."

The falling object had buried itself in the snow so quickly that we could not see what it was, but concluded it could only have been some small rock detached from the mountain overhead, and falling by chance into the gulf that had practically swallowed us. Jabez, though, was not content with suppositions. After the manner of his race, he determined to investigate this performance by digging out whatever had presumed to intrude itself into his own special domain. He was hard at it when another object fell, striking the balloon squarely on top, and bounding off into a deep drift of snow on the other side. A spume of feathery particles was displaced by the impact of this falling body, and Jabez's attention being attracted thereby, he made for it with furious barks, not,

however, until he had dug out the first meteoric visitor, and flung it with a growl and a shake of the head against the wall. Again there was a sharp, metallic ring, and Hill sprang forward.

"Good heavens!" he exclaimed, picking it up, "it 's an ice-ax!"

"Then what on earth was that big thing that dropped into the next drift?"

We hurried over to the spot, looking anxiously up for further foreign visitors. Jabez had answered the question. The snow was flying over his back as we approached, but seeing us, he at once stopped his vigorous digging, seized something between his teeth, and pulled at it with all his might. It was a piece of Scotch tweed of a tan plaid pattern, and it was attached to some resisting body. Hill took one look at it before we fell to digging, too.

"English," said he, "I 'll bet a keg of nails!"

# III

WELL, we dug him out. He was quite motionless at first; in fact, I rather thought he was dead; but Hill said no, only unconscious from shock—no bones broken, no outward injury that we could see.

"Nothing but his feelings hurt," said our authority on ballooning and excavations. His suit was plaid, his boots were of the most approved pattern, his calves fairly bawled from their pens. He looked as if he had just jumped off a bike or out of a golfing link, and there was a string attached to a buttonhole that cried monocle to the icicles.

"English to his toes," said Hill, regarding him speculatively. "If you don't believe it, just wait until he opens his mouth."

"I should like to see him open his eyes

first," said I, for our visitor was young and fair, and I did not like to see him lying in our gully like a log.

"Oh, he 's all right," said Hill, slangily. His spirits seemed to have revived wonderfully with this arrival. "Give him time, man. It 's all most men need to pay their debts in this world."

I helped him along with a drop of brandy, and presently he opened his eyes and looked at us. Then he sat up, brushing the snow from his clothes with feeble finger-tips.

"Aw—thanks, awfully," he said in a far-away voice. He seemed dazed yet, and he fumbled in his pockets and brought out a little flat wallet. From it he presently extracted with a shaking thumb and finger a round bit of glass, which he proceeded to thread like a needle, tying a knot in the end of the black cord that had been dangling from his lapel. As nearly as we could judge, the only loss he had sustained beyond the temporary damage to consciousness had been that of his eye-glass. Directly that was threaded and fixed up he screwed it into his eye and took a look at us.

"By Jove!" he said.

He next noticed Jabez, who was sniffing about him in the most friendly fashion,

"A BIT OF GLASS WHICH HE PROCEEDED TO THREAD."

wagging his stump of a tail, and he patted his head and said:

"Hello, old chap!  A bit of a mongrel, eh?"

His attention next wandered to the *Cloud Queen*, and he became transfixed. He gaped at it for a moment, then riveted his eyes upon the boat, and after examining it minutely exclaimed:

"How very extraordinary!"

He then arose, staggered over to the boat, knocked on it with his knuckles to assure himself that it was real, all the time exclaiming, "How very extraordinary!" and finally gave it a feeble shake, being himself in a very feeble and shaky condition as yet.

"Talk about ballooning!" said Hill. "This beats it all out of sight. Just look at that chap; he thinks he is in eternity. The last lucid thought he had was that he was on the edge of the end of all things earthly, and he's trying to adjust his ideas to dogs and boats in the next world. He has always been taught that the former had no souls, and that it would be too hot for the latter."

But pretty soon he came back, recovering his manners and his sensation of still being himself at the same time.

"I say," said he, hauling off his knitted cap, and holding out his hand, "it was awfully good of you to be down here,

"IT 'S AWFULLY GOOD OF YOU."

don't you know.  Whatever would have become of me without your opportune assistance I—aw—I—really I—aw—can't at all imagine."

"That 's right," said Hill, shaking hands with him cordially.  "We did not really arrange to be here on account of your coming, but if we had n't been I guess your name would have been Dennis all right."

The young fellow straightened up, dived into his pocket, fished out the wallet again, and drew forth a card.

"My name is Clambor," he said stiffly, "Lord Clambor."

"Delighted to see you, my lord," said Hill, taking the card.  "My friend Holdem of Chicago, Lord Clambor."

The young lord regarded me through his glass, and then held out his hand. Society at the bottom of a crack in the Alps could n't help being democratic.

"Feel any appetite?" Hill inquired.

"Well, rather!" responded our visitor, with an unmistakable emphasis.

"Suppose we sit down to lunch, then,"

said Hill, acting as master of ceremonies, and as cordial as if, with only three days' rations left, the addition of a new boarder did not reduce his own chances for life very materially. While we sat at lunch, the new-comer doing hearty service, Hill explained our situation, and the young lord gave an account of himself.

"You see," said he, "it all happened like this. I was tied in between two guides, but I slipped and fell, and the rope broke. Deuced awkward, don't you know —nothing to hang on to."

"Could n't you throw a rope over the atmosphere?" inquired Hill, innocently. Lord Clambor stared at him abstrusely.

"I suppose," said he, "I should have tried Mont Blanc first."

"What did you try first?" asked Hill.

"Well, I 've had a little practice, don't you know, but I doubt if any practice is enough. I 've been up Fujiyama, and part way up Kinchinjunga. But everything else is child's play to the Matterhorn."

"The Matterhorn!" exclaimed Hill.

"The Matterhorn!" cried I.

"Yes," said Lord Clambor, placidly spreading some raspberry jam on a piece of bread; "they say the Shoulder on the Matterhorn is about as nasty a bit of work as you want.   Mont Blanc is the thing to do first, you know."

Hill leaned against the side of the boat with his mouth open, and I suppose I did something equally intelligent.   Presently, as my companion seemed quite speechless, I inquired:

"Would you mind telling us what you fell off?"

"I really can't give you the exact spot," the young lord answered pleasantly.   "It takes it out of a fellow so, don't you know. I was quite knocked up by it."

"Knocked up or knocked down," said Hill, recovering himself, "is all one.   What was the name of the pile of ground you tumbled from?"

"Oh, you mean the mountain?   The Matterhorn, of course.   I started from Zermatt this morning."

"Comets and calculations!" shouted my friend, staring hard at the new arrival,—

who adjusted his eye-glass to bear a strain, and inspected him inquiringly in return,— "where are we at?"

The arrangement of this conundrum was manifestly far beyond the Englishman's powers of imagination, and as for Hill, he was dumfounded. He jumped up and paced nervously back and forth in front of the boat, winking very fast, and gnawing the ends of his fingers, as he did sometimes in moments of great perplexity. Pretty soon he stopped in front of me, and propounded:

"Holdem, what was the last thing you saw up above?"

"Mont Blanc," replied I, stoically. I meant to stick to my mountain when it was no harder to do than that. Hill resumed his striding, winking faster than ever. His fingers were in positive peril, but he was not yet satisfied. Again he wheeled around, propounding:

"Jabez, what did you see?"

Jabez cocked one ear up, and looked at his questioner unwinkingly for a moment. Then he twisted around and gave his attention to an old flea-bite far down on his spine where it was hard to get at. I never saw contempt for human conclusions shown more promptly or with greater comprehensiveness.

"That settles it," said Hill. "That dog has got more sense than we have. It 's just as I said—he knows better than to trust to his eyes alone. He would have to hear Mont Blanc and smell Mont Blanc before he said ' Mont Blanc.'"

Lord Clambor looked at us as though he thought we had all gone crazy.

"For heaven's sake, let us smoke, or do something," Hill went on, sitting down. "A good dense smoke might clear the atmosphere around us. You see," he said frankly to the Englishman, "we thought we had fallen into Mont Blanc."

"Fancy!"

"We thought we saw it as we came down. We had been up eight miles."

"Oh, I say!"

"It 's a fact, though. I 've got the instruments to prove it. That 's where we frosted our noses."

For a moment Lord Clambor's countenance almost showed an expression, but he checked it in time to save the monocle.

"How very extraordinary! Why, I thought it was port."

"No," said Hill; "it's frost-bite. Now, my lord, you have had some experience in mountain-climbing,—in going up and down mountains,—and you were kind enough to fetch your ice-ax along. Just cast your mountaineering eye over our surroundings, and tell me what you think of the chances of climbing out of this place."

Lord Clambor looked up at the ribbon of sky overhead, bright with the noon sun, and pretty nearly as thin as the edge of a goblet. He walked up and down the gorge some little distance, far enough to command a view of the end, and then he asked:

"Have you explored the whole length?"

"Yes."

"Is it all as bad as this?"

"Or worse."

Lord Clambor sat down, looking very thoughtful.

"My idea is," said Hill, "that it might

be done at a hazard and with great peril by cutting out steps as we climb, but the trouble is that a man's strength could not hold out to get anywhere near the top. He would have to cut a little, and return, and let another take his place. We would have to take turns, and it would be long and tiresome work; but if it is to be done at all, it must be undertaken at once; we have no time to lose."

"Quite so," agreed our new companion.

"The worst of it is that our provision is getting low, and we shall have to go on short rations. I should say that a man needed full-fed strength for that sort of work—although no man knows what he can endure until he is tried. I 've had some experience in climbing clouds, but very little climbing mountains."

"Quite so."

"As I explained, there is not enough electrical power left in the storage battery to get us up with the balloon. I hate like sixty to leave it here." He looked over at the *Cloud Queen* with a sigh. "That 's the best balloon that ever floated."

"It must have cost a pretty penny," said Lord Clambor.

"It did—a number of them, and several good-looking American dollars, too. In fact, like the American heiress, it 's made of dollars. I can see them now."

A glimmer of real interest passed over the face behind the monocle, and the glass itself was never trained upon any object with greater care. Its wearer sighted over at that balloon as painstakingly as any Chinese gunner in the late war ever squinted through one of the bamboo sights he had adjusted to a Krupp gun.

"If this fracture we are in happened to be in Alaska," Hill resumed, "I suppose that side of it would presently chip off and become an iceberg. But it is n't in Alaska; and as the only opening in life just now seems to be unsuited to our talents, we may as well begin making our own tracks out. I 've heard of people making tracks before."

"Hill," I remonstrated, "I believe the situation has gone to your head. You seem to me to be a little flighty."

"Well, maybe it has; I should say the situation was strong enough; and as to being flighty, I 'd like to be flighty enough to get out of this with the *Cloud Queen*, I can tell you!"

I was seriously alarmed over his mental condition, and Lord Clambor looked as if he was, too. We arranged that we should begin cutting at once, and that I, as the least experienced in the work, should undertake to hew out the lowest flight, thereby getting some practice for the more difficult labor of cutting and climbing higher up. Moreover, it was necessary for us to improve every moment of day-light, for the nights were cruelly long. We selected what seemed to be the most advantageous point in the ice-gorge, and I began my work. Heavens! what a task it was! I cannot undertake to say how often I dropped my ax in the course of the first twenty feet up. It was necessary to cut diagonally, but we decided to keep the angle as sharp as possible, thereby reducing the distance to be gone over. And how hard it was to cut each niche in the right place and at the right angle!   Often a great piece of ice would chip away—a deep sliver that left no place for another niche, but compelled an entire change of direction.   These accidents made us mindful of the fact that a piece of imperfect ice large enough to include the three little footholds to which the man who was cutting had to cling with fingers and toes might also be detached by a blow.   It was slow work and sober work, and when I came down from my first attempt, with muscles trembling from exertion, and looked up at the little flight of shallow steps—so long they had seemed to me, made at the cost of such wearisome effort—and saw that they covered only a fraction of the great wall stretching pitilessly away to that little thread of blue at the top, I sat down utterly discouraged.

"It never can be done!" I said with conviction.

"That 's what every one said about the Matterhorn," responded Hill, cheerily; "but by and by along came some men who did it, and we are going to do this."

"IT NEVER CAN BE DONE!"

I think I was the only one in the party who really gave up. The Englishman held on to hope with the regulation Johnny-never-let-go grip that a Britisher holds on to everything with. As for Hill, his spirit was so marvelous that I really did entertain doubts as to his sanity. His whimsicalities grew in proportion as our situation became more serious. The second night after we began our cutting I was awakened by the sound of tapping and tinkling, tinkling and tapping, down the gorge; and opening my eyes, I saw that Hill had rigged a candle to his cap after the fashion of a miner, and was working high up on the wall like a firefly on the bark of a tree. The icy gorge caught and repeated this feeble little light, every projection sparkling and glittering with innumerable repetitions of it until the whole narrow crevasse was turned into a Shisha Mahal—a Hall of Mirrors—fit to place in a king's palace. It was a pretty sight, but not one to take pleasure in, for I knew that Hill was in danger. The worst of it was that he was whistling away merrily some light, tripping air with a lilt and a swing to it like a Hungarian dance. We were in absolute darkness in the boat below, and I had no means of knowing whether Lord Clambor was awake, but presently he moved and spoke:

"By Jove! That 's what I call jolly plucky."

"It 's what I call a piece of idiotic daring," I retorted. I was touchy; and my nerves were getting strung higher and higher. "It 's all very well going up, but how in the name of Sam Patch is he going to get back? That 's what I should like to know."

And, as if in answer to my question, the light above suddenly went out. There was a splintering, grinding sound that detonated through the gorge like a cannon, and then a crash. After that all was silent. My heart fairly stopped beating, and Lord Clambor and I rolled out of the boat and stumbled down the gorge together, forgetting in our haste and fright that we could do very little toward discovering the body of our friend in the darkness. Jabez ran ahead, filling the place with echoes from his barks.

I shall never forget the horror of the next few minutes. The darkness of the grave I shall some day fill will be no more dense and impenetrable than the Stygian glooms through which we plowed along with outstretched hands, running against each other, bruising ourselves on the walls we could not see, and at last stumbling upon a new obstruction in the gorge. Jabez never for a moment ceased to bark, and the whole place seemed full of hollow echoes, a sort of weird thrumming of muffled sound from some gigantic string. Lord Clambor struck a match, and by the aid of two or three we groped around until we found the ax, that had fallen on one side of a mass of glittering ice, two or three tons at least, some of it powdered and pounded into snow as if the sides of the crevasse had been a huge mòrtar, and the law of gravitation the pestle hammering it down. It was useless to try to look for poor Hill. It would have exhausted every match we had and all our candles.

8

We might have to eat them yet before we were out of that dreadful place; besides, no human shape could have survived such a fall. That alone would have stricken life out, but to be pinned under that great heel of ice like a spider under a boot—well, he was in his grave. For the matter of that, we were probably in ours, too. There was nothing to say as we slowly groped our way back and clambered into the boat again. The chill of the place got hold of me with the nervous horror, and I shivered as if with ague. The very blood in my veins seemed turned to ice—the awful imprisoning ice around us, above us, and beneath us.

"Take some brandy, old chap," said Lord Clambor, kindly, "and don't give out. We 're jolly bad off, but we 've got to keep up."

I thanked him in a whisper, and complied. It was good advice, and the chill presently passed; but I lay there unable to sleep, tormented by my thoughts and by strange sounds that I had never heard before. It seemed as if the echoes of our footsteps, of the stumbling rush we had made down the gorge, the uproar of Jabez's barking, and our own few horrified exclamations, had twisted themselves together, and were also groping and rolling between the walls to escape, struggling to reach that top so far away. These sounds seemed living, incarnate, sweeping by with unmistakable evidence now and then, and again dying away in mysterious rustlings and breathings as of faint winds high up. The effect was ghostly and uncanny in the extreme. Even the dog seemed uneasy. He did not again curl up beside me as he had done before, but running my hand over him in the dark, I was aware that he was sitting on end, rigid and intent, all his faculties centered upon the one sense of hearing, too.

" I say, do you hear anything?" Lord Clambor asked.

Hear anything! I should think I did; but I temporized. Instead of answering his question I asked another.

" Do you?"

"Well, rather! I've been hearing something ever since we came back and were quiet."

"So have I," I answered then; "but I think it is the echo of all the crash and noise, caught high up and still reverberating." But there were ripples and crawlings over my cuticle that gave the lie to this, and chills were racing round my spinal column as mice or squirrels race in a tread-wheel. And just as my hair was creeping under my cap like a sturdy in a sheep's brain, Jabez burst into a dozen barks and leaped from the boat. If there are any further sensations of fright and nervous apprehension of ghostly visitants from another world to be experienced, I trust I may be spared the experiencing. Lord Clambor confided to me afterward that he was not in such a funk falling off the Matterhorn. And just as we were on the point of expiring on account of a supposed ghost, a match was scratched outside the boat, and illuminated—Hill! Hill, with a large and lifelike smile—it could n't be other than large, being lifelike. Jabez was defying gravity around him, and gamboling in the snow like an early spring lamb. Never tell me that dogs do not know what they are about. No man was ever welcomed back from the jaws of death by his best friend the way Hill was applauded out of the crack of doom by Jabez—an acquaintance of a week!

Yes, there was Hill; and in order to be absolutely natural he threw a switch, or touched a button, one—I never could tell by the looks just what he did. Now I had fumbled among those buttons when we got back from the supposed grave of Hill, thinking that a light would be cheerful in our darkness, literal and spiritual; but I might as well have fumbled among my own buttons so far as any results were concerned. A pile of dead ashes in an alley would have illuminated as well as I did; but the minute Hill put his finger on it, presto, change! the dry wand of my effort burst into the bud of his performance, or the full bloom, rather, for the light-gun was firing off fireworks as if in celebration of his return. I am not quite clear in my mind what happened then. I know that I rolled over the side of the boat into the midst of a leaping and cavorting Jabez, and fell upon his neck (Hill's, not the dog's), and that Lord Clambor, as guiltless of an eye-glass as he was at his birth, seized him by the hand and worked it as if he had a contract to pump the ocean dry, and Hill's arm was the handle.

"Why, I called to you," said Hill, "but between you two and Jabez you were making such a hullabaloo you did n't hear. And when I saw you scratching matches, and taking on over what you thought was my grave, I concluded I had better climb down from my perch before I yelled 'Morning!' like a cock-sparrow. I decided, too, that if I dropped I 'd drop easy, for I considered it would be taking a mean advantage of friendship to die twice on your hands. Why, what 's the matter with you two fellows? You both look as if you had seen a ghost. Now I want to tell you right here that we are going to get out of this. Just reckon up the situation if you don't believe it. Here are two men who have tumbled eight miles out of the clouds and landed right side up with care. How 's that?  Why, out of a million men who die a million deaths you could n't pick out two who had such provocation, or who would have been so justified by posterity in their departure.  I speak of ourselves first, my lord, because we were the pioneers down here.  Date has to come before title—in a crevasse, at least."

Lord Clambor actually laughed.  I shall always believe it was because he had been too much excited to put on his eye-glass.

"And here," continued Hill, waving his hand as if Clambor was the spectacle and the Alps were the spectators, "here is a man who has come a cropper off the Matterhorn, and failed to break his neck—failed to come up to expectation and comply with the rules of the game.  Does it look as if he was born to be hanged—as if a rope had any chance against a mountain?  Now I submit to you, gentlemen; *does* it look as if we were born to be drowned?  Well, I rather guess not!  It

looks to me more like we were being saved
to become presidents and prime ministers,
eh? But all this argument is n't worth the
forty winks we must get before daylight.
Turn in, everybody.   Lights out!"

# IV

IT was the earliest, dimmest kind of
dawn in our crevasse next morning
when I was awakened by the sound of a
terrific report.   My first thought was that
the balloon had exploded in some unaccountable way; but on opening my eyes I
perceived that there was a singular red glow
on the ice-walls ahead of us, apparently
about a hundred feet down the gorge.   Hill
was gone, and so was Jabez.

"What is that?" asked Clambor, in
alarm, as we started up together.

"Heaven knows," I replied.   "I suppose it's Hill somehow or some way at the
bottom of it."   I shouted his name, but he
did not answer; and as we were both seriously alarmed by this silence and the preceding explosion, to say nothing of the
unearthly illumination before us, we started

with one accord, as we had done the night before, and hurried in the direction of the light. I could hear Jabez barking, and presently he ran to meet us, only to turn and rush clamoring back in the greatest excitement.

"He acts as if something was wrong," remarked Lord Clambor. It seemed to me as if this statement was uncalled for, because, according to my understanding of the existing circumstances, everything was wrong, to begin with; but I had neither time nor inclination for argument. Almost immediately we beheld Hill staggering toward us, silhouetted darkly against the red glow behind him. The next moment he fell forward upon his knees, and from there lurched over slowly, easing himself down with one hand, like a man whose senses leave him gradually. Rushing to him, we found him lying with eyes wide open, in a dazed or semiconscious condition, and with several small, trifling cuts upon his face and hands. Jabez was whining and looking unhappy beside him. But what chiefly riveted my attention was the beatific expression on the fallen man's countenance. It was nothing short of seraphic.

" Hill, Hill!" I cried, " are you hurt?"

He looked at me dreamily for a moment, and then ejaculated:

" By the great horned spoon!"

Lord Clambor and I exchanged glances as we tried to raise him up. I thought he was raving, but directly we touched him he remonstrated peevishly:

" Let me alone! Let me be, can't you? I 'll get up when I 'm ready."

" But what is the matter?" I persisted. " What is that light? How did you get hurt, or if you are not hurt, what are you lying here for?"

" I 'm not hurt," he retorted in reply to my quadruple question. " I 'm just lying here giving my heart a chance to beat, that 's all." As he said it he raised himself rather uncertainly, rubbing his head with one hand as he did so—an habitual movement with him when confronted by some brain-splitting problem. Then he went on: " Listen to it! You fellows go down the gorge, and tell me what you think of that."

We were aware of an unusual sound in the crevasse, a noise like the sustained expulsion of breath from a pair of mighty lungs; and finding that Hill was not in need of assistance, we hurried to the spot. It was the same place where we had believed our friend had fallen the night before, and we now discovered that in our previous excitement and the surrounding darkness we had overlooked a great sliver of rock that had been split from the foot of the wall by the mass of descending ice, revealing a little cavern behind it. In the farthermost corner of this a great flame flared, a torch as big as a man's arm, burning fiercely, with that hissing roar peculiar to gas under pressure. I heard Hill's uncertain steps behind us, and turned to him. The little cavern was red and lurid, and reflected its glow upon our faces and the opposite cliff, where the ice was rosy as a snow-mountain at sunrise. We might have been three fiends holding consultation in the inferno.

"By Jove!" said Clambor. "How very extraordinary!"

"What in the world is that?" I asked.

"That," said Hill, looking dreamily at the flame, "that is gas—natural gas, right here in the Alps. Think of it!"

"But how did you happen to discover it?"

"I did n't," said he, grinning. "It discovered me, and the first thing it did when it found me was to kick me out with businesslike precision. By George! it pretty nearly jolted the life out of me, too." He stretched his arms and legs stiffly, rubbing them here and there, and wincing and grimacing as he did so. But presently he straightened up, forgetting all about his aches and pains in the excitement of a thought.

"Say! Talk about fortunes! If the confounded thing was anywhere else, just think of the stock company we could form! You see, when I awoke this morning early, I concluded to explore that part of the crevasse I had tried to knock over last night, and the first thing I ran across was this cavern. I thought maybe it might have chipped off the door to some other crevasse, through which we might perhaps crawl out, so I walked in and struck a match to look around. That was all there was to it : everything else just happened itself." Considering what *had* happened, this was deliciously droll, and he went on with a twinkle in his eye : " Now I want you fellows to turn in and make snowballs—big ones, fit to build a fort of. You 've not forgotten how to roll them up, have you, Holdem ? "

" I should say not; but what on earth do you want of snowballs ? "

" Well, I intend to put that light out the first act—not until it has melted a few barrels of water off that opposite wall, though. Then I shall build a flue of ice and snow, cemented with water, say three quarters of the way up to the balloon, using the sides and floor of the cavern for two sides of the chimney, and arching the third side of the triangle between them. We will bank the mouth of the chimney with stone to protect the snow and ice from melting too quickly, make a hole through the plugging of the fissure mouth, join it with the flue by cementing it over in a hurry, and light up our gas again just where we want it. Why, an hour of that heat—maybe half an hour—reasonably near to the balloon would thaw it. I tell you I feel good. Of course there is this objection to the scheme: if the heat required to float the *Cloud Queen* is also enough to float that avalanche overhead, we will have to tie to the ice-ax again for a life-preserver. But I believe luck is with us, and I propose to go right on making preparations to depart by first balloon. It's the easiest way out, and judged from my experience last night, it may be the only way. Now I want these snow-plugs made as big as barrels. It's going to be a ticklish job to put out that light, but I guess we can do it."

We ate our frugal breakfast first, with the thought that there was just enough left in the larder for one more scanty meal to act as an aid to digestion. So far as any prospects of a future dinner were concerned, we might have been the family of any brotherhood-bound striking workman.

The only satisfaction we had was that the world outside, like a walking delegate, was dining well.

During all that day we made snowballs, rolling them up and down the gorge, assisted by Jabez, who thought this exercise was devised for his entertainment. Big as our great torch appeared to be, examination showed that the fissure through which the gas came was a small, jagged, triangular rent in the rock, not above eighteen inches from the floor of the cavern. We experienced far less trouble extinguishing the flame than we had anticipated, and, barring some singed eyebrows and whiskers, Hill's plan of operations succeeded admirably. But it was long, slow work building a flue of the length required, and cementing every little irregularity that might perhaps allow the gas to escape, particularly as after a few hours it became necessary for Clambor and myself to explore the gorge from end to end for snow. Hill acted as mason, and we were " hod-carriers," according to him.

It was in the course of these explora-

"WE MADE SNOWBALLS."

9

tions that I came upon a curious piece of rock that had been at some preceding age grooved out by falling water, so that one side was shaped not unlike the half of a sewer-pipe divided longitudinally.   It was perhaps three feet long, and from one to two thick, very irregular in outline, of course, but I at once saw that it would be a valuable adjunct for finishing the mouth of the flue, where the flame would create an intense heat.   With Clambor's aid I carried it to Hill.

"Magnificent!"   cried   that   worthy. "Just the thing I have been longing for and wondering how I was going to do without.   Now look at it—just look at it, and dare to be pessimistic!   Why, I call it flying in the face of Providence—no less— to grumble at anything so far.   Have n't we been provided with everything heart could wish?—except, perhaps, a ladder out, and that has not been offered because we are not going to require it.   But some people are never satisfied; must have a chromo with their box of soap, or they won't wash."

We helped to place our find at a suitable

distance from the balloon, and by banking it high with rocks about the mouth we soon had a surprisingly good vent, in which the gas could burn for some time before it melted away the granite opening of our prostrate chimney.

Late in the afternoon we divided our last crumbs. I shared mine with Jabez, and we were both hungry after our banquet. At this time the flue was over half made, and we continued to work on it by candle-light all that night, being reasonably sure that the fissure was sealed well enough to prevent the gas from escaping in any considerable quantities. Next morning Hill melted some snow, and invited us to " come to hot water," requesting his guests to bring their own " spirits," and recommending that we make believe, as children do, that we were merely dyspeptic, and restricted to this diet for the sake of health instead of necessity. It was a pretty thin breakfast after twenty-four hours of steady toil, but our host reassured us by promising the best dinner to be had in Switzerland, served at twelve sharp.

"No fashionable hour for us," said he, briskly. "A good feed to-day, and welcome to fashion to-morrow."

It was while we were going through the empty form of this meal that Lord Clambor called our attention to Jabez.

"Look at that beggar," he said. "I never saw any one thrive on short rations the way he does. He is actually putting on flesh."

" In other words, this climate and dietary seem to agree with him," said Hill, " which only goes to sustain my theory that the mind has more to do with health and happiness than the body. Jabez has not argued himself into hopelessness, as you have, Holdem. He is going on the principle that 'sufficient unto the day is the evil thereof.' "

But a sudden suspicion had crossed my mind. I·knew Jabez well, and now that my attention was called to him, I perceived that he was filled with something besides hopefulness. There were attendant symptoms other than those visible to the eye in his increased circumference. In the first place, he did not tease.   That meant, with Jabez, " I am not hungry."   I knew that he had been very hungry only a little while before, and I marveled in consequence. Then, too, Jabez carried a red napkin in his mouth that he invariably used after meals.   This napkin was now doing good service, and when, after licking his chops to his satisfaction, he rolled over on his back and writhed around as he was wont to do from sheer excess of contentment at really possessing his dinner beyond the possibility of its being taken away from him, I sprang up.

" What in the name of heaven has that dog found to eat ? "

We started as one man in the direction from whence he had come last, and he, scenting discovery, ran ahead, looking back apprehensively now and then, as any provident-minded dog does when he fears his buried bone is about to be scented out by another dog.   We were all so eager that we forgot our anxiety concerning the glacier overhead, and at last we ran Jabez to earth in the little cavern where our big gas-light had been burning.  One side of this cave was of ice, and the heat had melted it away for three or four feet, as it had the cliff on the opposite side.  Here Jabez sat on guard, wagging his tail, and at the same time showing his teeth as one who would say:

"Now you see it.  Take a good look at it, but let it alone."

The shout we sent up might have started a dozen avalanches, for here was breakfast—aye, and dinner, too, and any number of meals, providing we were unfortunate enough to need them there.  Nobody knows how long the ice had been accumulating, but when the heat had worn it away the sharp nose of the dog had discovered what we should have failed to find—the carcass of a pack-mule, swept off the pass of Mont Cervin, perhaps, and preserved as if by Providence in this great refrigerator, for the needs of three little human things crawling around the spot long afterward. The circumstance of this discovery added to Hill's fund of cheerfulness.

"There," said he, "does that look as

if luck had deserted us? Better people than we have been reduced to rations of mule-meat before now. Of course, if this animal had been really thoughtful, he would have brought some green-groceries along in his pack, in which event we might have enjoyed our own garden here, so to speak. But we won't quarrel with our bread and butter—even if it is nothing but plain, ungarnished mule. You see, we are bound to get out of this predicament."

"By Jove!" said Lord Clambor, with enthusiasm, "I believe you are right."

"I know I am," said Hill, modestly, casting a speculative eye aloft. "We have nothing to fear now, except our enemy up there. If he will kindly hold off, and not take advantage of our defense-less position—"

But he was interrupted by a rumble and a roar, a crash as if heaven and earth were smiting together, and we all sprang to our feet and looked into one another's white faces.

"What 's that?" I asked when the tumult had subsided.

Hill had seated himself almost immediately, and now said in a careless, offhand way, as if such a trifling circumstance hardly merited an explanation:

"That? Oh, that's probably just another Englishman dropping in."

Clambor was getting in a measure accustomed to Hill's pleasantries, but the voice with which he got off his regulation retort, "Oh, I say!" was decidedly feeble.

"Sounds to me as if he had brought his whole island along," pursued Hill, cheerfully.

But the humor of the situation had rather a pallid color. I knew and Hill knew—we all knew—that if the accumulated snow on the mighty roof over our little house was sliding off the eaves in one place, there was no reason why it should not slide in another at any moment. Damocles' sword was a puny instrument of destruction compared to the one hanging suspended over our heads.

There are a few things—raindrops, microbes, gray hairs, and troubles—that never come singly. And sometimes one piece of good luck pairs off with another, and there you have the beginning of a jolly family party in time. We finished our breakfast of mule-steak—Hill said we could call it beef if it would make it taste any better—feeling our spirits reviving with every mouthful, and our confidence in the future returning in jumps. Sixty minutes later we had the connection made between the fissure and the flue, and had the gas lighted again, this time without accident of any sort. In an incredibly short time it became apparent that the balloon was reviving, too. Poor old *Cloud Queen!* She was getting the chill out of her bones and straightening up again, preparing once more to soar into her own domain. To say we rejoiced is a feeble way of expressing it. As for Hill, he fairly wept. He ran over at the first motion of the great dull body, and took hold of a chain here and a chain there lovingly, as if they had been the hands of a friend he had thought dead miraculously restored to him; and he talked encouragingly to it, as though his words were understood and were helpful. Then he rushed back to the boat.

"Come, now," he cried, seizing it vig-

orously, "with a will!   We have no time
to spare."

We took hold of it as men do when man-
ning a life-boat, and we pushed it over the
intervening space as the crew shoves the
craft they may perhaps be about to lose
their lives in—or save lives—into the surf.

"We can't wait, or hold her back with
stay-lines until the ascending power re-
gains its full force," said Hill; "it would n't
be safe.   Besides, going up slowly will be
our salvation.   It 's the only way of getting the *Cloud Queen* out without damage
that might ruin her."

We were attaching the chains to the boat
as he talked, and we could see that they
were gradually straightening out.

"Get in, get in; wait for nothing!" cried
Hill.

Lord Clambor jumped first, and Jabez
and I followed.   Hill ran back for the
ice-ax.  .As he returned I saw him start
and throw his hand up to his head.   When
he reached the side of the boat there was
a little cut on his temple from which the
blood trickled slowly.

"GET IN! GET IN!"

"Nothing but an icicle," he remarked cheerfully, " and a small one, fortunately."

But we all knew the significance of that falling bit of ice.   As the man stood there, with his hand on the taffrail, and his head thrown back to look at the balloon above us, I thought that never before had any human being lived in whom the spirit predominated so absolutely over the flesh. His face expressed only a keen and comprehensive interest in the workings of the mechanism he had invented, and he was watching the process of ascension with the same careful professional attention he would have given it if he were preparing to ascend from any dooryard in France. It was the finest piece of absolute self-control in the face of imminent danger that I ever saw.   We knew that, so far as our chances went, we might just as well be sitting over a mine of gunpowder to which the fuse was laid and lighted, cheerfully hoping that the spark would expire before it reached the bulk of destruction.   Clambor looked at our chief intently and steadily, but his face will never be more bloodless than it was then.

"Ah," said Hill, pleasantly, "she floats at last." He gave the boat a slight push, and I perceived that we had indeed cleared the bottom of the gorge.

"For heaven's sake, get in!" I stammered. I felt that he would be quite capable, in that debonair, careless fashion of his, of letting us go without him if he found at the last moment that the balloon would not carry us all. Some suspicion of this crossed Clambor's mind, too. The color came back to his face with a rush, and he sprang up like the gentleman he was.

"I say," he cried, "none of that! If any one stays, I do."

"No, you don't," said I, feeling miserably mean to have him speak first. "Both your lives are worth something, and you have other folks to think of. I 've nobody but Jabez, and if anybody remains, we do —don't we, Jabez?"

Now I know that dog understood what I said and what my words meant just as well as if he had been human. He looked up at me seriously, shutting his lolling mouth the better to hear, and after a moment's affectionate scrutiny he clambered up on my knee and licked my face. But Hill helped us over an awkward pause.

" No heroics booked for this trip—thank you both, just the same. We can't spare anybody; our party is too small. But Jabez is the last man that goes. Why, Jabez is our mascot, eh, old boy ?" He gave him a friendly pat, but the dog looked sober and leaned hard against me, running his tongue out and back rapidly, as if he was searching around in his mouth for the right word, but could n't quite get hold of it. He snuffled, too, and that was always a mark of deep feeling with Jabez. Altogether, I knew he had expressed himself something like this:

" That 's all right, thank you. I appreciate your attention, and I entertain the highest opinion of you as a gentleman and a fakir. I 'm glad to stay, too; but it would have been just as master said. I stand by master in everything. He 's the only man I know who is always absolutely right on all subjects."

To our great relief, Hill's additional

weight did not appear very materially to affect the upward tendency of the balloon, but, horns of the Alps! how it crawled! When I thought of the way we had shot up through space the day we left Chamonix, and compared it to the way we crabbed along now, it was maddening, even though I knew that in this slow progress lay our safety *if* the avalanche held off. But what a big word those two letters made just then!

As we arose, and I looked back upon our prison with its trampled snow and ice, through which ran the mark left by the boat like the trail of a great snake, while on the other side glowed and streamed our banner of flame with its fringe of ascending smoke, I perceived that under our north wall there was a little jagged, wet trench, like that under a dripping house-eave in a thaw. Only this line curved and wound in and out with a sinuous, menacing, serpentine fashion like something alive, and moving according to its own erratic notions instead of tamely following the straight line of a carpenter's wall. This sight would not have added to any feeling of security we might have had, and in the silence of the next few minutes there was a sound equally disquieting ascending to us—the sound of a sputtering hiss now and then, as drops of water from above splashed into the flame below.   Water was also falling from the top of the balloon and trickling down the chains and valve-rope, and there was ever that monotonous drip, drip, drip on the floor of the cavern, seeming to our excited imaginations to be steadily increasing in volume.   Patter, patter, patter came the sound, like hundreds of fleet steps following us—steps of sprites and gnomes who dwell in habitations unknown to man, and resent his advent into their domains. Drip, drip, patter, patter—it was a veritable quickstep.   All the trolls of the eternal hills were after us to drag us back.   It seemed to me, as I lifted my horrified eyes away from the slowly increasing depth beneath to the strip of widening sky above, where the edges of the crevasse stretched like wide lips in a horrid, fiendish grin at our presumption, that we were literally in the mouth of the mountain.   The question was, would the great jaws close upon us and crush us?   And as we rose higher and higher and approached the top, I could see the glacier hanging curled over the grinning lip like a cruel, lolling tongue waiting to lick us into the maw of eternity.

Now it would be bad enough to be roasted, or smothered, or crushed, or frozen. Any of these words set by reality as a period to life smacks of the tragic.   But to be roasted, *and* smothered, *and* crushed, *and* frozen makes a combination death that rises into the realms of a disaster alto-gether too complex to be appreciated by any plain, unaspiring individual.   Few persons want a death constructed on the composite order.   At any rate, I never should select anything so ornate as that for my own demise; my tastes were always simple.   But that was just what our pros-pects seemed to be for a few minutes, as we soared lazily out of that awful gulf. How green its walls were!—green or blue, as you choose to call it—like grotesque cliffs of petrified sea-water—of deep-sea water,

10

frozen and split asunder by some caprice of nature, filling an idle day with the ruin of an earthquake or the orchestra of a cyclone.

The top of the balloon had evidently reached the level of the crevasse. We saw its huge shadow darkening the front of the suspended cataract above us. Leaning over the edge of the boat and looking up with suspended breath, we saw this shadow suddenly careen violently to one side. The next moment the *Cloud Queen* was flung against the inanimate pile of carved and statuesque snow, chiseled thus by the savage tools of those wandering mountain sculptors and climbers, the untrammeled winds. We had been on the point of deliverance; we had caught breath to cheer; but now each man grasped the sides of the boat and waited in silence. The good craft we were in was raking upward with violent jerks and plunges, as if the *Cloud Queen* was struggling with some mighty enemy to preserve her own life and the lives of her human cargo. Pieces of broken crust flaked off the snowy wall within reach of our hands and fell crumbling upon us. And then we saw the great white river begin to move; slowly, sluggishly, with the creak of rending ice and the groaning grunt of some huge animal goaded and lashed into reluctant motion. And we—we were jerked out of the vortex into which that frozen torrent began to pour ever faster and faster, like puppets on a string, up into the sunshine, into the sweet air, out of that well filled with noisome gases, but into a wind that bore us along like a feebly resisting feather over that rolling, roaring Niagara into which it seemed we must inevitably be plunged. The *Cloud Queen* had risen out of the grave, only to be smitten by the mighty palm of a hurricane and driven like a frightened bird against the ragged walls of the Matterhorn, or engulfed in the icy torrent below. A ghostly spume of snow rose from it as the resistless force of gravitation hurried it on, and the opposing winds plowed into it with savage thrusts and plunges of gusty strength. The great airship dipped and rose, rose and dipped, until at times we shut our eyes, feeling that the

"WE WERE JERKED OUT OF THE VORTEX."

next instant would see us wrenched out of the air and tossed into the awful chaos of that entombing stream. With its thunder in our ears, and the fear of it in our hearts, we passed what seemed an eternity of time, expecting each moment to be blotted out of existence as completely as if we had never been.

# V

I SAW Hill's lips move two or three times, but it was impossible to hear a word in the uproar by which we seemed engulfed. Have you ever seen a withered leaf caught in the angle of some big building, and hurled hither and thither, round and round, up and down, almost dropped, perhaps skimming the surface of the ground in search of some peaceful spot on which to rest, and then caught up again and hurled on high, a plaything for the autumn winds? Well, that was precisely the position we were in for what seemed a cycle of time. In reality I suppose not more than a minute or two really elapsed before the crashing roar beneath died away and the last of the avalanche disappeared down the mountain-side. Beneath us, where that strange rushing field had been but a moment before, there lay a great jagged trough, a furrow plowed out by a power before which iron would have been but paper and steel like wisps of straw. And then, as if the forces of the air lost interest as soon as the great dance was ended, the winds passed in a howling gust, after driving us with but moderate force against the towering wall of the mountain. Here a precipice rose above us, straight and tall, and against this the balloon was lightly tossed now and then, rebounding like a ball, but drawn back again to the rocky cliff as if by a magnet. Probably that was the secret of the unaccountable attraction the *Cloud Queen* exhibited for the earth in preference to the air—an attraction that forced us to be constantly on the alert to push the craft away from projecting points of rock toward which we were continually being drawn perilously near. This slow, seemingly cautious ascent gave the balloon the appearance of feeling its way like a person giddy with the height above and depth beneath; and it did not take us long to realize that we were enjoying a unique experience, even though our nerves were somewhat shaken. As for Hill, he revived from danger as a gull does from a dash of spray, and events that would have turned an ordinary man's hair white seemed to him unworthy any special comment.

" How 's this ? " he asked Clambor, pushing the boat away from an arm of rock that seemed reaching for it. " Does n't this beat your method of climbing? "

" Well, rather!"

" Less exertion required, and, according to my way of thinking, less anxiety."

" Wait a bit," said I. " You may call this trip free from anxieties; but if I get back alive I mean to pay the premium on my accident policy with humble gratitude and my congratulations to the company."

Hill looked at me quizzically, and nodded to Clambor.

" Pretty poor performance, that, on the fiddle-string of friendship, eh? Here I 've pulled him through everything so far, and yet he expresses doubts as to my ability. There 's nothing like judging a man's future by his past. However, Jabez and I don't worry, do we, Jabez?"

Being aroused from a slight slumber by this question and the prod of a boot-heel, Jabez wagged consent at once—but he was a bit of a wag anyway. He then for the first time became aware of the vicinity of the mountain, and he at once sized it up as a trespasser, and pounced upon it accordingly.

"Can't you read a sign when you see it?" he indignantly inquired of the Matterhorn. "What does 'Keep off the grass' mean, anyhow? 'Come and sit down'? Well, I rather guess not! You 'd better go to school, you had."

Jabez paused, but the mountain maintained a haughty silence which irritated him, and he went on:

"I 've had my eye on you for some time, and I wish to say right now that of all the ugly-looking mugs I ever saw, yours is the best specimen of that kind of architecture. Wow! Go off and hang yourself to something high, and get out of the way!"

I had often encouraged Jabez to express himself freely, but I had more than once had occasion to lament his tendency to drop at once into personalities.  He ought to have edited a city daily or been a politician.  I could see that he was working himself up to a pitch of profanity, and I tried to calm him.  This timely effort would no doubt have succeeded had not the edge of the boat caught just then upon a sharp projection of rock beyond Hill's reach.  In an instant Jabez had it by the throat.

"You miserable, Castle Garden importation, you," he growled.  "What do you get for your vote, anyhow—fifty cents, eh?  And when you 've floated it on a deluded democracy, you don't know whether you 've voted for justice of the peace or president of the Guatemalan republic, do you?"  (Jabez thought he was shaking the mountain savagely, but it was himself chiefly.)  "You 're a pretty specimen of darkest Africa to be let loose in a civilized world, you are!  I 'll teach you the difference between a good, free, stand-up-and-fight democracy and a sit-down-and-die-

away European monarchy before I 'm
through with you—see if I don't."

Just then the balloon wrenched us free,
and Jabez was flung violently to the bottom
of the boat. He picked himself up at once,
and scrambled to the side, where he supported himself with his fore-paws, panting
with rage.

"You just do that again, if you want me
to give you what for! You 'll want to
crawl into your kennel and die when I get
through with you next time."

"Go for him, Jabez," said Hill, encouragingly. "Don't you hesitate to tell that
Matterhorn fellow what you think of him.
You ease your feelings and hurt his all you
want to, and I 'll keep the price of board
down just as if nothing had happened."

I suppose that men who had climbed up
by foot and hand to where we were would
not have been in a very hilarious mood.
I could imagine the way they would have
felt by the way I felt trying to climb out
of the crevasse and cutting my steps as I
went. That method is pretty hard grub-
bing. It 's like comparing the struggles of

the worm to the flight of the butterfly, and most any one will admit that crawling is not to be compared to flying. But ballooning goes to your head; it 's intoxicating; and I could understand how Hill had grown to the point of absolute physical superiority to fear of airy distances and depths, through familiarity with them and many successful ascents and descents. I knew this to be his position,—I had seen it demonstrated,—and I aspired to share it, although I knew that I could not so easily shake off that bugaboo of mankind, the fear of death.

" Let 's have a look," said Clambor, intently studying the map of rock and glacier and precipice below us. Presently he pointed to a spot some little distance down. " I think it must have been about there I lost my footing and began to slide. By Jove! it 's deuced uncomfortable to think my mother and sisters at home believe I 've been lost in some awful way here in the Alps. They did n't want me to do the Matterhorn."

" You mean they did n't want the Matterhorn to do you," amended Hill. " But you will probably find out that every one thinks a great deal more of you now than they did before your demise—and that 's not intended as any reflection on you or on their affectional powers. It 's the way of the world. A man has to die to find out how much he is really worth in cash and character—and then others find it out, not he. It amounts to this, that a man never can get a proper estimate of himself."

" Quite so," assented Lord Clambor, readily, and he seemed wonderfully cheered by this view of the case. I concluded that perhaps some English maiden on whom his young affections were riveted might have been obdurate—until she knew he had fallen off the Matterhorn. Women are like that sometimes. When a man is here they wish him somewhere else ; and when he 's dead at last they want him back again. At any rate, dead or alive, they like him none the worse for having done something really big, and Lord Clambor certainly had. We had seen him do it and could witness his claim.

We were now at that portion of the final precipice guarding the top of the mountain, from which four of the seven men composing the first party ever making a successful ascent up that terrible height had fallen to destruction while descending. Such toll the giant claimed of those who passed his gate of victory failing to read the sign:

" Here thou shalt not."

Above us were the overhanging turrets of the monster's castle, and below us a drop of nearly a mile on to the glacier's hard bed. Now and then we passed bits of rope attached to the rocks, blackened as frosted ferns, and tasseled with icicles from whose tips the water dripped in the sun. Thin, glass-like ice clung to corners where the heat had not yet penetrated, while the exposed points were wet and warm, steaming in the cold air as the south slant of a roof will in a February thaw. The thought that little human things were ambitious to crawl over that stony countenance, to play hide-and-seek with death in the frowns of that awful face, where a false step would flirt them into eternity as if the giant shook his head, was appalling to me. But it made the true sportsman's blood in Lord Clambor's veins tingle with enthusiasm. He exclaimed. He was enchanted. He even forgot his monocle; and the passage of expression over his physiognomy, disturbing surfaces unaccustomed to it (like the big Alpine face before us), displaced the glass, and it fell continually like loosened rocks from the mountain's face.

"St. George and the dragon!" he cried presently, "this is what I call ripping fine sport."

"How does it compare with golf?" asked Hill, blandly.

"Well, you know it 's different—quite different."

"Does n't work in links, eh? Now there 's polo, for instance: how does polo compare with ballooning?"

But I interrupted. I did not propose to have the young lord quizzed into another facial paralysis.

"I should say those two sports were about alike so far as promise of a broken neck is concerned. You can do it in either game, ballooning or polo. Exceptional facilities offered in 'steeplechasing, too."

" Quite so," agreed Clambor, evidently relieved.

" Now," cried Hill, abruptly, leaning out and looking up, " take a last look at Zermatt and the Gorner Grat, for we are going to inspect Italy next.   Gentlemen, I congratulate you upon having done what no man has ever accomplished before you: you have made the ascent of the Matterhorn in a boat!"

Hardly had his words reached our ears, and the realization of what they meant made itself clear to us than we were on the ridge of the mountain.   As every one knows, the top of the Matterhorn bears the same relation to the rest of it that the spinal column bears to the bulk of the human body.   But there is this difference: the body of the Matterhorn slopes away sheer and precipitate from the narrow line of its backbone, so to speak.   Our boat caught, and for a few moments we looked along that uninviting ledge of schistose rock and snow, no wider in some places

than the saddle of a hobby-horse, and
gnarled as the knuckles of age. It was
literally a ledge of rock seemingly resting
on the air, a sliver of terra firma uptilted
into space, and apparently defying gravitation and every law ascribed by the finite
to the infinite mind as contrived to preserve the equilibrium of terrestrial things.
Hill swung a switch, and I knew by the
sound that he had lowered the anchor-
claw.

"You may as well get out," he said airily
—as might have been expected. "This
boat touches here to discharge cargo and
load. Ten minutes' stop for inspection.
Trading or bartering with the natives prohibited."

I had never felt any mountainward-soar-
ing ambition, so I merely put one leg over
and touched my toes to earth. It was
enough to justify any statement I might
wish to make thereafter about having actually "set foot" on the Matterhorn. But
Lord Clambor scrambled out eagerly, and
began collecting pieces of rock. He had
filled one pocket when Hill said to me:

11

"I wonder if he is thinking of taking home a load from this quarry — enough to build an ancestral hall, or something?"

Jabez had looked over the edge of the boat, and decided there was no attraction for him in the lay of that land, at which he sniffed suspiciously; and when our English visitor came on board once more we were ready to weigh anchor and sail on. But by one of those contrarieties of fate by which persons depending upon electricity are sometimes annoyed, we did neither the one nor the other. We could neither weigh nor away. In vain Hill touched buttons and wielded switches. Like a penny-in-the-slot machine, we were out of order. The anchor-claw was overboard and gripping the Matterhorn like grim death. The cable that held it might have been filed, for it was not as big as a barrel nor as long as a crusader pedigree; but, like Mercutio's wound, it was "enough," for it was out of reach even if we had been provided with a file — which we were not. And cold! — gods of the arctic regions and snow-mountains, how cold it was! The thermometer did not say this, but we felt it keenly, for there was a bleak wind blowing, and it pierced to the bone. Moreover, we had been comparatively comfortable in the crevasse until we lighted the gas—or found it, rather. Then, what with our exertions and excitement, we had been far too warm. As a matter of fact, we were drenched with perspiration, and considering that Hill and I were both incased in two suits of the thickest procurable all-wool underwear, this was not surprising. We had not dared to lay off a pair, knowing we should need both directly we were out again. Lord Clambor wore thick silk and a knitted sweater under his jacket, so he was not so uncomfortably warm below, and naturally did not find it so freezingly cold above. Jabez, too, having been less inconvenienced by temperature of one kind, was not so susceptible to the change.

Hill took up some planks, and went to work in what would have been the hold if we 'd had one, and left us time to spare in the contemplation of our surroundings. There may be things or places in this world more beautiful than the panorama beneath us.    I have seen some spots in Japan that I thought lovelier than any known portion of the globe,— known to me, I mean to say, —and I have championed the Himalayas, and Darjeeling, with its glimpse of Kinchinjunga, many a time.    Also, I have waxed eloquent (after the third course) at many a dinner when I dwelt in memory upon the beauties of that hill of the Moors, —that European treasure-house of Oriental history in tangible form,— the Alhambra, with the Darro flowing under its walls, and the snowy Sierra Nevadas glimpsing the sky beyond it.    And then there is Ceylon, the Garden of Eden—but all these comparisons are futile.    There is no place like the Matterhorn.    I shall not try to describe it, for it would be impossible to do it justice.    Besides, we were viewing it under disadvantageous circumstances.    There we were, anchored to a rock, with no certainty of ever letting go our hold, with no spiked shoes or guides or ropes, with no lanterns, no experience, no toboggan—no nothing of anything that is usually considered essential to climbing up or down a cold, unsympathetic mountain like the Matterhorn. There was a certain anxiety connected with our position which any conservative man can understand. And all the while I did Hill full justice—as much justice as any man ever gets in this world. I took reasonable account of what he had done, but I held to the knowledge that human ingenuity is fallible, and that, however brilliant his achievements might have been in the past, there was no telling what disaster might overtake him yet.

So while he tinkered with his machinery Clambor and I looked at the world: at all the horns of the Alps—the Rimpfischhorn, the Breithorn, the Rothhorn, the Gabelhorn, none like the one that impaled us. We had not even the satisfaction of knowing that our dilemma had two horns, and that we were between. The Matterhorn was built like a rhinoceros, and we were fast to the business end. Our only comfort—and it was a cold one, as cold as a refrigerator-car—lay in our view. Mont Blanc towered over everything around it, a white mountain of grand proportions. Other peaks stood about like ninepins about a hunchback player. At one side there was a Niagara (reproduced upon a large scale) of clouds tumbling and boiling over a mountain damming the Italian skies, and these nebulous torrents, so tangible to the eye, melted suddenly into a different temperature, and vanished like some Lost River of the air.

Hill lifted his head presently to catch breath. "Don't go ashore again," he said. "If we ever get shut of this grab-bag game, we may leave suddenly, without blowing a whistle."

He continued to putter with his electrical apparatus, and we continued to contemplate the beauties of nature in lofty altitudes, for perhaps another quarter of an hour. No one seemed to feel communicative. It makes a difference in one's conversational ability whether one has anything to say or not. Speaking for myself, and I judged Clambor felt as I did, my intellectual energies were devoted to the problem of how we were going to get down in case the balloon could not be released. I did not see that we were any better off than we were in the crevasse. Then we were afraid that something was going to fall on us, and now we were afraid that we were going to fall on something. Neither Hill nor I were mountain-climbers, and Clambor's record was not distinguishing. He might better be listed with mountain-tumblers, and I could see by the anxious pucker in the brows over the monocle that he had small relish for a return to earth by pedestrian methods. In my own mind I suspected that, for a while at least, his nerve was pretty well shaken. As to Hill, he was not to be considered speculatively. He could be depended upon as being game to the last, and he might get the machine in shape—he had pulled us along so far. But I felt gloomy. Pretty soon he bobbed up again.

"Well," said he, "we may as well take our midday repast here as anywhere."

"I like that," said I, with my best ironical inflection, "considering the fact that we have nothing to repast on."

He looked at me for a moment with both eyes, and then he slowly and impressively shut one, and looked at me with the remainder of his optical equipment.

"You just hop out and gather a few icicles, won't you?  I 'll melt them for drinking material."

"I say," said Clambor, "let me."

"My young friend," remarked Hill, earnestly, "I have caught you on the fly once when you came flying down, and I have cheerfully assisted you to come flying up to our present exalted station in life.  I have done these things at great expense and with exceeding labor, but I protest against your getting up any further entertainment.  If you take a header from this quarter of the globe now it will be U P with you ; so compose yourself and sit still. But you "—to me—"you shatter your composure for a minute, and fetch me an armful of icicles.   I 'll have the steak ready in a jiffy."

"Steak!" exclaimed Clambor.

"Steak!" yelled I.

"Steak!" barked Jabez.

"You did n't suppose I was going to come away from any such refrigeration as that with an empty larder, did you?  Our bill of fare might be more varied, gentlemen, but I doubt if it could be more sustaining."  He opened a little cupboard where he had stored the provisions when we had any, and having lighted the grid-iron, as he called it, proceeded to lay a big mule-steak upon it.

"Why," said I, as I crawled cautiously overboard, "I have been thinking what fools we were to come off without a mouthful."

"I 'm not such a fool as I look," retorted Hill.  "Will you get those icicles, or won't you?"

I finally managed to get out,—feeling curiously stiff in the joints, which I attributed to sitting still so long,—and started icicle-hunting.  I soon found that it was not safe for me to try to walk on that narrow ledge, because of giddiness; so I sat down astride, and hitched along slowly.  The wind was rising, and as I worked away from the boat, it seemed to pierce the side of my body most exposed to it with sharp, hornet-like stings.

"Look sharp!" shouted Clambor. "If he stumbles you 'll come a deuce of a cropper."

"Keep a tight rein," yelled Hill. "If he kicks up you 're a goner."

They were having a good time at my expense, and I thought if it pleased them it certainly did not displease me. An occasional appetizing smell of roasted flesh was wafted to me, and it did a great deal toward keeping me in good humor. I suspected it also raised their spirits.

"I say, is n't he going to bolt?"

"Somebody head off that mule—he 's got the bit between his teeth."

"I saw Buffalo Bill in London, don't you know; and upon my word, he exhibited nothing like this. He had some ripping rough riders, too."

"Ladies and gentlemen: you will now see an unequaled exhibition of skill and daring by Texas Tuck, the world-renowned and only King of the Bucking Bronco Steerers, rounding up a herd of icicles

"KEEP A TIGHT REIN."

over a piece of the roughest riding in the world."

"You fellows can come out here and round up your own icicles in about one minute—if I hear much more of your cheek," said I.  I had my pockets full of young and presumably tender specimens, and two or three big, hard-shelled samples were under my arm, so I concluded to turn around and go back.  They both gave me the benefit of their advice over this movement.

"Pull hard on the right rein, and grip tight with your knees," contributed Clambor.

"You 'd better tack to leeward," hailed Hill.  "Take in a reef, and try not to run us down."

I scrambled up to a wider place and turned around.  It was wide enough for me to lose sight of the precipice below, and I felt I could shake my fist at the mockers without shaking myself off the mountain; so I did it with all the muscle I could muster.  The process of lifting my arm was exceedingly tiresome, and as to getting up and down as I had been obliged to do in order to accomplish the turn, I was amazed to see that the stiffness I had at first noticed chiefly in my joints now seemed to extend all over me. My back might have been eighty years old, so far as its youthful spring was concerned. But I managed to start back without accident. The *Cloud Queen*, glittering like a silver corselet, and showing glimpses of changing color between the links of fine metal lace, was swaying in the freshening breeze as gracefully as a lily on its stalk. I could see the anchor-claw gripped on a boulder below, and the boat itself grazed the top of the mountain and shone resplendently. Flashes of light from its mirror-like surface dazzled my eyes as the sunshine caught it; and what with the blue above and the distance and depth all around, it was a magnificent spectacle. Hill and Lord Clambor grinned like demons over the side, and Jabez had his pointed nose aimed at me as it rested between his paws.

"You 'll need some patching done when you get home," said Hill, as I drew alongside. "I should say the effects of that exercise would beat cellar doors all to pieces." He reached over the edge and relieved me of the icicles under my arm, and I contrived with great effort to climb back unassisted. Then I emptied my pockets of their cold cargo, and rolled up in my blanket. Hill melted an icicle, poured in some brandy, and served it all round.

"Grog it is when tea it is not," said he, with unimpaired cheerfulness. He kept up a continuous fire of funning all through the meal, and when it was finished went back to work on his machinery smoking like a chimney. We found solace in tobacco, too, but I could not get the idea of my strange sensations out of my head, and conversation languished on my part. The wind blew ever fiercer and fiercer, and our position was becoming more and more unpleasant. In case of any phenomenal disturbance of the air, the balloon might be beaten down against the rocks, torn to pieces, perhaps blown clean away from the boat. In any event, that meant an immediate capsizing of our craft and an indiscriminate spilling of passengers down the mountain-side. In lulls of the increasing gale we could hear detonations of varying degrees of sound below, where detached boulders started on their rounds of echoing leaps, touching the earth at intervals with explosive pops like the discharging of guns. These died away in the abysmal depths below, and according as they were big or little, few or many, they resembled the sharp rattle of small arms, the boom of big guns, the roaring of artillery, or the all-enveloping thunders of an avalanche. Clouds began to roll around us as we poised perilously on the topmost brink. The world was shut away, and we seemed to be the focusing-point of an Alpine blizzard, in whose thick snows the *Cloud Queen* was lost to sight above, as the farthermost parts of a ship melt into nothingness in a fog at sea.

THE violence of the storm abated after a couple of hours, and then the snow fell gently, bringing the darkness with it. I never saw such flakes. If Mother Winter was picking her geese in the cold clouds above us, she owned a remarkable flock. Judged by the size of the feathers on the Matterhorn, her geese must have been ostriches. These huge flakes fell softly about us, obliterating the rocks, and changing the outline of the knife-back of earth to which we were moored. After a time this also ceased; but the moon and stars were obliterated by dense clouds. Hill had succeeded in getting all his electrical contrivances in order, except the anchor-claw, of course. We could have done without all the others, and naturally they were what we had at our disposal. It was cheerful, however, to have the light-gun to fire into the darkness around us. It turned the mountain into a lighthouse, and, we afterward learned, carried consternation into the towns below, where people forsook their beds to marvel and wonder if a star had fallen and caught upon the peak—a star whose light was often obscured by drifting clouds. Every guide within sight started that night to make the ascent and investigate the phenomena, and one party already *en route* turned back under the impression that the Matterhorn was developing volcanic symptoms. I asked Hill what effect he thought the light-balls would have upon the imaginations of the inhabitants, and he said:

"None whatever. They probably look no bigger than lightning-bugs at this distance."

"But they move," I persisted, "and I believe they are reflected upon the clouds beyond and increased until they present a very noticeable illumination."

In point of fact this was actually the case, and the light-gun of the *Cloud Queen* revived those old legends concerning the City of Demons on the peak—that ghostly city superstitious folk believed in until human eyes had actually seen the top at close quarters.    Even then there were those who said that a phantom city could not be visible in the sun, anyhow; but had not they themselves seen it—tower and battlement, wall and dome, uplifted often and often against the skies, tipped with roseate hues at sunrise, or standing black and grim against the clouds at night?  Of course; they had seen it with their own eyes. And now strange will-o'-the-wisp lights streamed from this goblin stronghold. Perhaps the cycle had come round,—the hundred years or thousand years,—the gala anniversary time when the castle was gay with the ghost of beauty, and the fortress was manned by shadowy yeomanry whose thin blades dazzled weirdly in the moon.    For the moon was rising over some white shoulder of the Alps, and like a silver sea the clouds melted before her.  The sight was magnificent beyond description.

I had noticed that Hill had been quiet

for some time, talking but little, though when he did speak it was in his usual happy-go-lucky style.   I had hesitated to say anything concerning my own feelings, for I felt we had enough to worry about without adding any new and inexplicable ailment of one of us to the situation.   We had managed to rig a blanket over the boat during the snow-storm, and this we had taken off, shaken as well as we could, and when it came time to go to sleep we had tried to wrap up as usual.   I was half dead for sleep, and yet I was unable to move hand or foot, and the knowledge of this kept me from closing my eyes.

"We will have to help Jabez keep dog-watches through the night," said Hill.   I felt that I could remain silent no longer.

"Hill," said I, "I 'm sorry to say any-thing about it, but there is something wrong with me."

"The deuce, you say!"

"No, I did n't say the deuce, but I feel deuced queer."

"E'gad!   I 've been feeling that way myself for the last twelve hours."

"You don't say!"

"It 's a fact, though. Lord Clambor, are you O. K.?"

"Never more fit in my life, bar nothing but too much appetite for too little dinner."

"Jabez," said I, "come out here, you beggar. How do *you* feel?"

Jabez came wriggling out from under the blanket, and I saw at a glance that he was in possession of all his faculties. I drew a sigh of relief. Thank heaven, we had two able-bodied passengers! We all looked at each other, and I could see Clambor's eye-glass fairly twinkling with interest.

"I say," said he to Hill, "are you feeling seedy?"

"Seedy!" retorted Hill. "I 've gone to seed. I 'm nothing but a dry and lifeless pod. I can turn my head and my wrists, and wriggle my fingers, but that is the end of my abilities."

"By Jove!" exclaimed Clambor, genuinely alarmed. The monocle glittered in the moon like the diamond-crusted hilt of Excalibur in the eyes of good Sir Bedivere.

He looked apprehensively at me, and Hill said judicially:

"Holdem, state your symptoms."

"I have n't any," said I; "I have n't a symptom to hang a statement on. I have no pain, I think as clearly as ever, I see as well as ever, my mouth does not taste livery; but I 've had a stroke. I can turn my head as you can, and have the use of my hands as you have, but otherwise I 'm a dead man."

"How very extraordinary!" exclaimed Clambor.

"Yes," I went on; "I 've either had a stroke, or else I 'm frozen to death and don't know it."

"Same way with me," said Hill. "I expect it was exposure in that confounded crevasse."

"Oh," groaned I, not with pain, but mental anguish, "they say death by freezing is painless. Maybe that 's what ails us."

Clambor unrolled, and went to first one and then the other. He felt us over carefully, and tried to take our pulses. I suppose he wanted to do something professional to cheer us up.

" Aw," said he, with due deliberation, " you—aw—you can't be frozen, you know.  You 're warm."

" Do you know anything about medicine?" I asked.  He was obliged to admit that he did not.  It was like his British cheek to give an opinion about something he knew nothing at all about.  Was n't science always making new discoveries?  Were not medical reports always full of unprecedented cases and diseases that the medicos had to think up new names for?  And freaks—were there any prospects of ever getting to an end with freaks?  How, then, did he presume to say that we were not frozen just because we were warm?  Mighty little he knew about it!  But he wrapped us up in blankets just as if he thought they would do us good, and went on with his asinine driveling.

" On the other hand, you are not feverish.  I 've had fever myself,—a jolly bad spell of it, too,—so I know it is n't fever."

Fever!    Two men dead from frost and yet suspected, even, of having fever!

"Do you think you could let me see your tongue?" Clambor next asked me.

"LET ME SEE YOUR TONGUE."

Idiot!    But I knew he had his hands full with us both, so I was willing to gratify him to that extent if it would make him feel any better.    It could do me no harm, even exposing it to the night air like that.    He did not know how to shoot with our light-gun, so he scratched a match, and burned the brimstone under my nose while he examined that tongue as if he were trying to decipher hieroglyphics on an obelisk. He would have looked wise and made me keep my mouth open until I had chilled my lungs and added pneumonia to my other miseries, had not Jabez taken an interest in the examination, and tried to crawl down my throat, which gave me an excuse to shut my mouth without appearing rude. But when Clambor scrambled over to Hill on his errand of mercy, and scratched another match to illuminate another tongue, Hill was rude.

"Get out!" said he, not considering the difficulties attending that instruction if Clambor tried to follow it. "You would n't know a human tongue from a pickled sheep's or a smoked beef's if you saw all three on a plate together. I won't have any man but a dentist prying into my mouth, and I never had one of them try it but I came within an ace of knocking him into the middle of next week. My tongue is all right, my lord. You can tell that by the sound—O shades of the great departed!"

I never heard an able-bodied seaman express himself more fluently and eloquently than Hill did during the next six hours. I should have remonstrated with him if his expressions had not agreed so perfectly with my sentiments. As for the Englishman, if he was shocked he managed to conceal it. I could not make out whether it was natural politeness or profanity welling up in him.

"I wish you 'd punch some of these buttons for me," said Hill to Clambor, as viciously as if they had been heads. Under his instructions, Clambor fired off the light-gun, and also turned on the current under the gridiron. Then, Hill acting as *chef*, and Clambor as a sort of scullery-boy, he cooked the last of our mule-steak.

"We 've got to have breakfast now," Hill explained, "and we might just as well eat everything we have, for I 'm going to consume all the electricity in order to release that anchor-claw. It 's the only way. I hesitated to do it at first, because I did not want to exhaust our power, but there 's no use hesitating any longer. It 's our only chance to get off this blankety-blank mountain. I 've always wondered how a camel's hump felt, but it seems to me we are doing the hump act now with a vengeance." He trailed off into broken wanderings that I will not record.

We ate our breakfast at midnight, Clambor feeding us each in turn, like a big one-eyed robin bringing up a brood of phenomenally early birds. But I think to any discerning eye we would have resembled a nest of nightmares rather than a nest of nightingales or robins. We were as helpless as babes; and as a diet of meat and brandy had made our chief want that of something to drink, Clambor finally gave us each an icicle to suck, and Hill and I lay there and glared at each other, like a pair of bad-tempered, overgrown twins in a cradle trying to extract comfort from their bottles. Thus the night passed slowly, but about four o'clock we saw the balls from our light-gun, that had been constantly discharged into the darkness since twelve o'clock, fade gradually away; and after their disappearance there was a tinkle from our anchor-claw as its strength departed from it. The next moment we rose into the air and floated off, released at last.

Oh, the joy, the satisfaction, of that sensation! the pleasure of seeing that mountain receding over our stern! We felt as Prometheus would if Jupiter had said hocus-pocus over his liver and set him free. And then the sunrise! Catching its heavenly hues, and illuminating like a fleet at sea for some emperor's *fête*, the valley clouds rose around us, and we descended softly into them as if launched into a fairy ocean. But as the sun rose higher and higher, and the clouds dispersed, and it became necessary for Hill to take our bearings in order that we might make a proper descent, I perceived that he was merely a log like myself, with only the use of his head and his hands, all three members attached to immovable sticks, as mine were. Clambor executed all orders with cheerful alacrity, and manned the craft, under Hill's direction, as well as any one could, now that we had no complicated machinery to look after.  With the coming of daylight our English friend inspected us minutely, and after a deliberation that seemed truly medical he diagnosed our cases as paralysis.

"You be blessed!" said Hill, irreverently.  "I tell you, I am not paralyzed. Why, did you ever know a true case that did not extend to the mental faculties, and also affect the facial muscles?  Does this look like paralysis?"  He winked with his right eye, and then with his left.  "Or this?"  He elevated his frosted nose, off which the skin was peeling until it seemed to grow between his eyebrows like a Japanese pug's.  "Or this?"  He slid his ears up and down on his head, and wound up with a succession of the most awful distortions of countenance I ever looked at.

"Hill," said I, after I had watched this performance for a minute or two, "you could earn your living making faces for the public.  What the world wants is amusement, and I never saw so unique a talent hidden under such a bushel as yours before."

His eyes twinkled, and he took kindly to the idea.

"If I find out that I have ossified, or petrified, or done anything past revision up here, I 'll remember that suggestion and try to get a job making faces in a museum."

We had been so entertained by this exhibition that the balloon had been left to its own devices; but now, glancing ahead, we were horrified to see that we were approaching Mont Blanc at railroad speed. It was really Mont Blanc this time, and if we kept on there was no reason to doubt that we should strike about half-way up the mountain in very short order. I never saw Hill wink so fast, and I knew that all the repressed energy in his body had been transmitted to those lids.

"Throw all these seats overboard!" he shouted. Clambor tumbled us off unceremoniously, and did as directed. "Throw out the blankets!" again yelled Hill, seeing that no effect had been produced. "Throw out the dog—anything that is n't nailed down!"

Now when he said, "Throw out the

dog," Jabez knew what he meant as well as I did. He looked at Hill reproachfully, and then, the instinct of self-preservation being strong even in a dog, he tried to hide himself under me. But, fortunately for Jabez and his master, there was something else to do, for by the time the first articles had gone by the board Hill was shouting other orders:

"Pull the valve-rope! It 's no use trying to do anything else. Let the gas escape as quick as you can, and when we reach the ground the dangling anchor-claw will break our fall somewhat."

Clambor was adjusting his monocle and squinting around for the rope, but Hill was impatient. Like the average man, his temper was not improved by sickness and adversity.

"Oh, hang the eye-glass!" he shrieked. "Pull the rope, man! pull the rope! Look at that blankety mountain ahead!"

But it was too late. The next moment there was a crash, an explosion, and we were buried under a mass of fine chains and gasy-smelling silk. The balloon had been

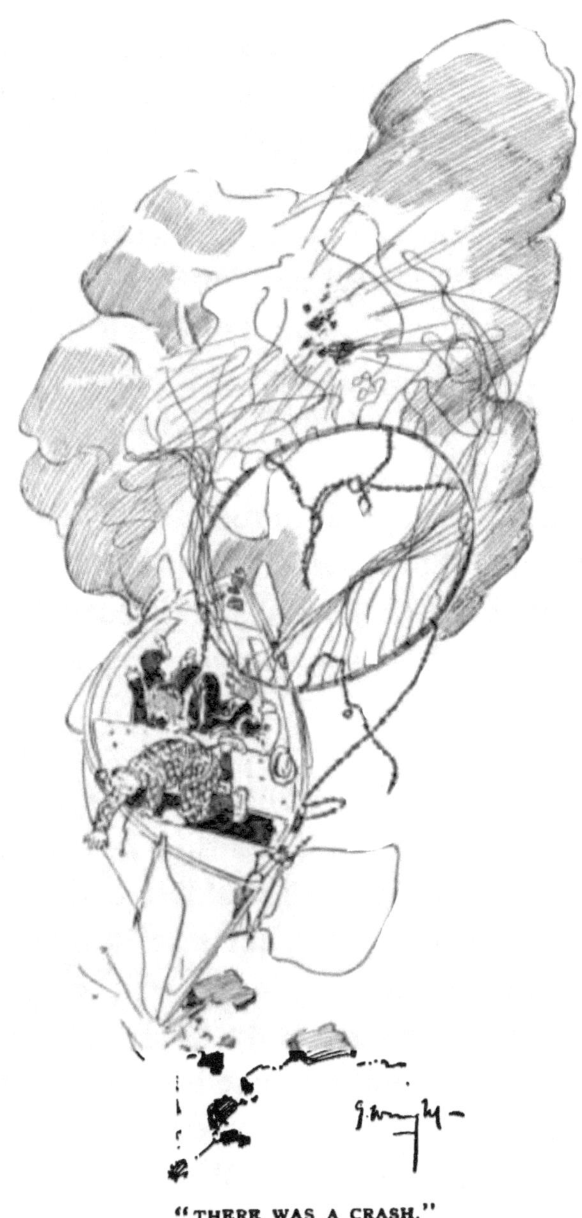

"THERE WAS A CRASH."

blown a few feet in advance of us, and I shall always think that saved our lives; for nothing but the mesh of chains over the top of the boat prevented us from being fired right at the mountain when the craft struck.   As it was, we were caught by the fallen mass of the balloon, which had itself hit a protecting boulder and collapsed with a big pop like an air-inflated paper bag on a large scale.

I have always admired nerve in a man, —probably because I have none too much of it myself,—and I have regarded Hill as the nerviest person of my acquaintance. But I must say that, for an Englishman, Clambor made a pretty good exhibition of that quality.   He struggled around until he had freed himself, and then he contrived to pull us up by the shoulders and give us air.   Jabez did not require assistance; for, after giving two or three yelps when the crash came, he speedily took account of himself, and finding that he was in good working order, he followed his nose out without loss of time.   We were moving, but not with the motionless ease of air-transportation. We seemed to be bumping along like a springless wagon over a bad road, but going at a good pace.

" What 's the matter now? " asked Hill, not nearly so tart as before. A danger passed always raised his spirits. It was then that Clambor rose in my estimation to sublime heights of nerve. He had made a wad of the balloon material to sit on, the seats being gone, and he now took a handkerchief out and polished his monocle as carefully and painstakingly as he ever did in his life. Then he put it on, and steadied himself by a hand on the side of the boat, for we seemed to be increasing our speed.

" I 'm blowed if we are not on the tail end of a blasted avalanche," he said, sulkily. But he was just as calm as if he had said, " We are in the Duke of Sutherland's conservatory." I could not help looking at him admiringly.

" Great guns! " cried Hill, his eyes sparkling. He thought a moment, and then exclaimed: " Well, that may be as good a way of getting down as we could wish — if we don't try any leap-frogging over some-

thing bigger than we are.  I did n't plan
the *Cloud Queen* with a view to playing
leap-frog, or doing any tobogganing or
snow-shoe act."

Lord Clambor looked as vexed as if he
thought we had put up that avalanche job
on him, and for a while he sulked like a
salmon.  Of course we did not expect him
ever to see a joke.  As for Jabez, he had
barked at the convent, at the clouds, at the
flag, at the crevasse, at the mountain, and he
now barked at the avalanche.  He barked
at it from the front, and the rear, and both
sides, and from which ever way he saw it,
he was unable to discern any virtue in
it.  In his opinion, it had a tumbled,
tousled, dissipated, just-been-out-all-night-
and-have-n't-combed sort of look that was
to the last degree disreputable.  So he
barked, and Lord Clambor sulked, and Hill
and I waited.

The chief objection to going avalanching
is that you never know when you are going to stop, or how; and as the same sort
of troubles beset you before starting, I
feel that I am safe in making the statement

that, in my judgment,—based upon experience,—there is nothing about it to warrant its ever becoming a popular pastime. But I have always advocated the theory that whatever is is for the best, and I felt more than justified in my belief by the final experiences of that trip. It very often happens that things we can only regret at the time, that seem especially calculated for our vexation or undoing, turn out to be the traditional disguised blessings. For instance, had Clambor pulled that valve-rope when Hill wanted him to, we should have dropped far afield in the avalanche, and been buried somewhere at the foot of the Alps to-day instead of pursuing our separate vocations (Clambor has none, but he 's married—and married to the girl who would n't have him before he fell off the Matterhorn) as we are. That delay in doing what seemed to be the best and wisest thing at the moment saved us. As it was, we jogged along with the anchor-claw and the balloon trailing after, and presently these caught on something we had bumped over, and we stopped with

"WE STOPPED WITH A JERK."

a jerk. Lord Clambor and Jabez took headers from where they were sitting, and Hill and I, in our plaster casts, catapulted out indiscriminately, and raked along a little way on our own account after we landed. But the avalanche had gone on.

I received a smart rap on the head from something we passed, and this rendered me unconscious for a few minutes. I remember coming hazily back, and getting a dim glimpse of Clambor at work over Hill. He had a knife in his hands, and had every appearance of being engaged in the operation of skinning him. A horrible thought that Hill was dead and Clambor gone mad flashed through my mind before I again lost consciousness. My next sensations were of blessed freedom, of restored strength and animation in my poor body. I jumped at the conclusion that I had died and gone to heaven; but the sound of unholy laughter and loud barking disabused my mind of that pleasant fiction. I judged I must be in the other place until I recognized Jabez's voice. Then I tried my arms; they moved. I tried my legs; they were alive. I concluded I would sit up, and I sat up.  Lord Clambor was holding his sides and shrieking with laughter; and Hill was trying to hold his sides and wipe his eyes at the same time, but he was a little stiff yet.  I looked at myself.  My hands were red and swollen, and my body was ribbed in red and white of a curiously familiar pattern.  A pile of small-sized, thick, shrunken-looking garments lay between Hill and me, and they were raveled and ragged where they had been cut, but they bore the same resemblance to the human body in their cast-off estate that a snake's skin does to his.

"Hill," said I, with a gasp,—I was beginning to comprehend our paralysis, our having been dead, but yet being alive,—"it—it was n't—"

"Yes, it was," gurgled Hill, between hysterical breaths; "all wool, and a yard wide, too."  He rolled over on his back, and writhed as if he had recovered the use of himself.

Clambor sat down on a stray rock, saying weakly, "Oh, I 'm blowed!"

He was, literally.  And while he wept for

joy, and we joined in, content that he had at last seen a joke, we also dressed by degrees, as our strength permitted, and Jabez barked and gamboled about like a dog gone mad. We were not even damaged; as Hill said, not even our feelings hurt.

So we trudged merrily to the nearest town. We had lost our balloon and our woolens, but what did it matter? We were ourselves intact, and we had been up the Matterhorn in a boat.

9 783954 272365